THE WILD WOLF'S WIFE

3 IN 1

MANDY ROSKO

The Wild Wolf's Wife Volumes 1, 2, and 3 Copyright © 2017 by Mandy Rosko

Cover Art by Melody Simmons

All rights reserved.

Produced in canada

ISBN-13: 978-1548631598

ISBN-10: 1548631590

No part of this book may be reproduced in any form or by any electronic or mechanical means, including information storage and retrieval systems, without written permission from the author, except for the use of brief quotations in a book review.

MANDYROSKO.COM

PATREON.COM/MANDYROSKO

Created with Vellum

DEDICATION

This one is dedicated to especially to the Beautiful Alphas who support me on Patreon. You guys are amazing, and I'm so proud that we made it to our second print volume. I can't wait until we can do this again, and I am so thankful to you for following me on this romantic reading experiment. This book is for you, even if you didn't want your name listed below :D Here's to many more! Happy Reading!

Nicole henry, Jessica Ripley, Denise McNamara, Susan Kay Ryan, Sherry Bruyette, Nancy McDonald, Toni lunt, Cynthia Claus,

Jessica Hoskins, Maritza Fleming, Michelle Fortune, johanna snodgrass, Alisha Derr, Teresa Ward, Sherry Smith

Tami Gryder, Shandra Torbett, Andi Downs, Christina Morgan, Monica Lynn Emery, Leanne Ede, Joyceann Tenney, Krista Jones, Cassandra Hyden, Stephanie Pittser

Leslie Gordon, Saleena Chamberlin, Christine abee, Ramona Cabrera, Dusty Weller, Terri Eaches, Sharon Bishop

Virginia Phillips, Roxanne Johnson, Kayla Reindl, Cheryl Viner, Karla Porter, Mary Szigeti, Rachel Morse, Karen, marlene eaton, Donna Hokanson, Julie Spencer, Annette, Selmeister, Wendy Custer, Crystal Graham, nina bajer, Lynne Norvell, annette alex, Doris Linton, April Woodward, Brandee Adriance, Jennifer Gaston, Carolyn Lown, Irene Lu, Mellissa, Maragaret Noble, Jill Micklich, Confused child, Samalee Johnson, Sandy Folz, Misschel Eldred, Janet Rodman, Jeanne Clark, David Friend, Sherilyn Cook, Kaer Baer, Tiffany Haskins

S.A. Buchanon (Printer), Alexandra Smith, Virginia Robinson, Donna Hogel, Nanci Quinn, Janice Richmond, William H., Stacey F, Barb Sands, Margaret Hobson, Marcy Schwendiman, Christina Dawson, Lori Trask, Kim Corriher, Charlotte Brincat, Sharon Manning-Lew, Alana Pike, Teresa Albarran, Tricia Wright, GerryAnn Lantto, Jeanie Filter, Amanda Barker, Angelina Bao, Linda Heredia, Katie Kruszka, Gail Powell, Rose Allen, Karen Large

RetiredHsMom, Denise Holder, Deborah Gillespie, Michelle Chantler, Maria T, Ramona M Pierce, Jennifer Booth, Donnie Bozeman, Lori Martin, Jacquie Piunti, Rachel Barckhaus, Rebekah Snyder, Sharron Anthony, KermitsGirl , Jean Eldred, Charz Moore, Alysha Parent, Lynne Cuda, Laura Furuta, Cathy Birkett, Angela Cowen, Diana Mason, Stephanie Paul, Sharon Hatt, Megan Mills, Susan Fuentes, Belinda Sweeney, Beth Wolfe, Kristen Lewis, Maria Willett, Sharon Chalk, Tara Wellington, Toni Mcconnell, Anne M Rindfliesch, Valerie Cobb, Valerie Jondahl, rachael ayers, Tiffany Villeda, Edith Chiong, Iona Stewart, Traceylyn Norrie, Corrina Mayall, Jamie Pittman, Ellen Swindall-Bailey, Valerie kendle, Patricia short, Alexis Abbott, Selena Kitt, Essie Munro, Anna Garcia-Centner, Cindy woolcott, Biggi Ziegler, Jill Morrison, Alexia Falco, Kerrin Brittain, Melissa bush, Jane Edmunds, Jerrianne Ray, Linda Barbala, Melanie Holm, Tamala Smith, Ruth Roberts, Claudia Beukmann, Yvonne Daniels, Andrea Belknap, Carol Ingham, Jacqueline Williams, Cynthia Powers, Tanya, Yolanda Pedroza, Mary Becker, Belinda Jarrell, Gwendolen Doffing-Waldrop, Tracey Moore, Miriam Loellgen, Vicki Johnson, Pam Van Veen, Tammy Francis, Valerie Marshman

CHAPTER 1

"And by next full moon, my foster son, Dempsey Walsh, will take the hand of Jolie in mating matrimony."

Jolie Farris blinked at the announcement read by the alpha from his iPad. She waited for Renzo to tell her it was a joke, but Renzo wasn't the type to joke, and the way he smiled softly up at everyone gathered around for pack announcements suggested he was being more than serious.

Despite being something of an asshole, and the sort who never cared about what anyone thought, their feelings, or anything that fell outside the category of safety, security, and food for the pack, he wasn't an asshole on purpose.

It just seemed to be his personality.

He was going to let Dempsey mate with her? He was going…but he didn't even ask her about this.

Dempsey. Holy shit. No way.

The pack clapped softly. Jolie looked at the faces around her. Many of the people here were ones whose couches she'd slept on, or spent time in their spare bedrooms over the years.

And yet they were clapping and looking as if what had just been announced was a good thing.

Or at least, not the absolute worst thing in the world to happen.

A few of the men even got up to shake Dempsey's hand and congratulate him. He'd been sitting near the front, but was now standing, ready to accept all the praise that came his way.

And when Dempsey looked back at her, that eager smile on his face, her skin crawled.

This wasn't right. She didn't want to be mated to him. She wanted nature to pick her mate and no one else. She already *had* a mate.

The women didn't get up, but the ones sitting around her did put their hands on her shoulders, their smiles approving.

Couldn't they tell she was not okay with this?

Jolie stuck her hand in the air.

Renzo noted her, and Jolie was shocked when he pointed his pen at her and called her name.

"Yes, Jolie?"

She'd half expected him to ignore her, knowing that she was about to object.

Jolie put her hand down. "What happens if I don't want Dempsey for a mate?"

The ladies, mostly omegas, and almost all of them mothers who didn't want trouble for their pups, turned away from her. They were no longer smiling at her with those looks of happiness. They looked more as if they wanted nothing to do with her if she was going to make a scene.

She didn't blame them for that.

"Do you object to Dempsey because you feel he cannot provide for you?"

"No," Jolie said.

Dempsey was totally watching her. She could see him

from the corner of her eye. She also did not want to look at him. She wasn't going to look at him and see his anger, or his disappointment.

He seriously thought they were made for each other.

"May I ask what the objection is then?"

"I don't want to."

Somehow, that should have been enough, and yet there Renzo stood, flicking that damned pen in his hand, as if he'd heard the most disappointing thing of the evening.

"Jolie, you are older than breeding age. It's time you had a mate."

"Okay, well, can I choose one for myself?"

"Dempsey will take care of you. He is a strong alpha, and he's had his eye on you for some time. He will not take advantage of you."

Jolie felt the little muscle beneath her eye start to twitch.

Don't glare. If she glared at him, she'd get smacked for it. And that was the gentle approach.

Betas and male omegas who glared got more than a smack across the face. She didn't want that, but she didn't want to get mated to Dempsey either.

Unlike Renzo, who seemed to be logical to a point of fault, Dempsey absolutely was an asshole on purpose.

To this day, Renzo couldn't make him stop putting out those bear traps for Liam.

Liam...

"Any other objections?" Renzo asked. He was an aging alpha, but still powerful. The gray and silver hair, and they way he pushed his reading glasses up his nose could lead some people to think it was easier to push him around than it actually was, but it wasn't that long ago when Renzo had killed another alpha, and he'd always proven his strength in the ring.

No one dared fight him on anything. Whether it was a physical fight, or an argument.

Jolie was in a mood to push her luck.

"What if I just don't like his personality?"

There were a few small hissing noises, as if people were having sympathy pains for what she was about to go through.

It was her own damned fault. If she got a small beating for this, then no one would stand up for her, and no one would stop it from happening.

Renzo glared softly at her. "You liking his personality has nothing to do with whether or not he can keep you fed in the winter."

"All he would have to do is get a job for that. He doesn't have to hunt our every meal."

"Then you agree to be mated to him on the condition he seeks out human employment?"

"What? No!"

"Then what is the problem? I'm losing my damned patience."

Renzo's eyes flashed a bright shade of red. His lips pulled back, revealing the sharp points of his fangs.

Yeah, he was definitely getting angry with her.

Without meaning to, Jolie looked towards Dempsey, who looked as if he was trying very hard not to glare at her, too.

If she pissed him off enough, would he want to mate with her? What would he do if she made his life miserable and tried to get him to walk back on the mating idea?

He might scar her face for daring to turn him down.

Jolie shivered. She wasn't getting anywhere with this, and she could practically feel the eyes of the others on her, watching her, some of whom were begging her to stop it, to quit while she was ahead.

Even the others in the meeting who weren't looking at her, she felt the thick press of their need for her to stop.

If she didn't, even if Dempsey decided not to take his anger out on her, he could still decide to make someone else's life miserable because of what she was doing.

No one really liked Dempsey, though everyone claimed to like him.

He was good-looking, a fair hunter, and if he ever got his own pack one day, he might make for a strong leader.

If anyone ever wanted to follow him. Somehow, Jolie got the impression that, in a past life, Dempsey would have made a fine Ramsey Bolton.

She was going to get herself hurt if she kept arguing this point.

"Well?" Renzo asked, his voice gruff, still impatient, and not angry.

Jolie swallowed hard. She looked over at Dempsey. He didn't look angry anymore. Just impatient to get this show on the road.

Jolie shook her head. "No."

"No objections?" Renzo prompted.

"No," Jolie said again, another soft shake of her head.

"Good. And don't put on that face. Most unmated wolves are paired off, and Dempsey will make it so that you and your pups never go hungry. That is a good thing."

Jolie nodded, because technically, Renzo was right. Hell, he'd probably taken that into account when Dempsey begged the man to hand over Jolie's hand.

Because Jolie had no doubt in her mind that was exactly how it had happened.

Renzo was like a second father to Dempsey, ever since Dempsey's father had been killed.

By Liam.

There was no telling how many times since Jolie had

turned seventeen that he'd begged and pleaded for her hand. She had no idea why. It wasn't as if they spent any time together, knew each other, or liked each other. He just thought he liked Jolie, and that was a problem.

And now Jolie had to think her way out of this, because opening her big mouth and arguing wasn't going to get her anywhere.

Liam. That was the best answer she could think of. She needed to find Liam.

He was still around, even though he wasn't supposed to be. They used to be friends, and he was already in trouble with Renzo and Dempsey, had been avoiding them for years...

Maybe, if she found him, and asked nicely, then for old time's sake, he could help her out?

That was a stretch.

Jolie knew Renzo was finishing off with the rest of the news for the pack, she could hear him, but her brain wasn't turning the sounds he made into words.

She was too busy making her plans, because there was no way in hell she was shacking up with Dempsey.

If he seriously thought she wasn't going to do anything about this, then he was a little dumber than she'd given him credit for.

Now it was just a matter of getting away from a group of alphas and betas who were ten times stronger, faster, and better trackers than one omega who didn't know when to shut up.

CHAPTER 2

Jolie Farris hissed as she sliced her palm open on what used to be a tree branch, but at some point it had fallen off, or had been broken off by roaming animals, leaving a spike for her to slice herself on.

She brought the bloody mess up to her mouth and sucked on it to ease the sting. Then she stopped, looking down at the blood that pooled in the cut.

Jolie pressed her lips together.

She could either use the blood and hope to attract her prey, or she would end up leaving a trail that Dempsey would be able to follow all too easily.

Double-edged sword. One way or another, this wasn't going to go her way, and someone was going to end up getting hurt.

Probably her, but that was what happened for not being an alpha, or even a beta.

Omegas didn't have the tough skin their counterparts did, and the sun wasn't even all the way down yet, but the heavy shade through the canopy above her made the temperature drop more and more.

She was getting cold, and hungry.

She honestly hadn't thought it would take so long to find him. Jolie had kind of hoped Liam would just be out here, waiting for her, and that after an hour of walking at the very most, she would stumble across him.

Or he would let her find him.

That didn't seem as if it would be happening now. She'd made a run from her pack four hours ago.

Jolie checked her Fit Bit.

Four and a half hours ago. She was totally screwed if that was the case. Dempsey was probably already out there, running through the woods, trying to catch up with her.

He would definitely catch up with her because he was an alpha. He didn't have his own pack, but he was definitely an alpha. Strong, thick-skulled, and didn't like taking orders from absolutely anyone.

And he wanted her to be his mate. Dempsey wanted Jolie for a mate, and Renzo had signed off on it.

Jolie pushed forward. If this took any longer, she was going to start yelling for Liam to show himself.

The way Dempsey constantly bitched about how he was always getting closer and closer to the territory, she would have thought Liam was constantly just a stone's throw away, but it turned out that wasn't the case.

He was close to the pack, but far enough away that an omega that didn't have the same skills and protections as a beta or an alpha would have trouble finding him.

She wished she'd worn a better coat for this. Thank God she'd put on her hiking boots. The only reason she didn't shift was because she needed to keep from losing her purse and wallet.

Clothes had a nasty habit of getting lost or torn up in a shift.

"Goddammit." Jolie stopped, putting her hands on her

hips, and then yanking her bloody hand away when she remembered it was bloody and she'd just ruined her jeans.

Jolie clenched her teeth. Bad day. She was having a bad day, and just because this probably wasn't going to work didn't mean she was going to sit back and do nothing while Dempsey decided she was going to carry his pups.

No. She wasn't going to do that.

Jolie pressed on. One aching foot in front of the other. That was the way this worked.

Until she caught the sound of a howl off in the distance.

Goosebumps prickled up all along her arms. The fine hairs on the back of her neck stood up and sizzled, as though jolted by electricity.

Jolie wet her lips. *Okay, think*. She was going to think about this instead of panicking.

She couldn't fight them off if they tried taking her back, but she could figure out where they were.

To the south of her, coming from the pack. That much was obvious just from the direction of the sound.

The distance put them at about ten minutes away. Fifteen if she was absolutely lucky.

Jolie ran. She'd already been running in spurts, getting sweaty and out of breath before walking, then starting that process all over again.

Now was as good a time as ever to start running.

She wasn't going to let herself get caught. She was going to fight this. Even if she had to fight a bunch of betas and alphas, even if she had to fight off Renzo and Dempsey together. Even if she had to stick her claws into their eyes, she wasn't going to let them take her back, and she wasn't going to let that son-of-a-bitch mount her and put his pups inside her.

No fucking way.

The next howl was closer, and Jolie had no idea what she

was running towards. She had no sign that Liam was even in the area. Jolie wasn't much of a tracker, and she just started walking in the direction she'd last heard he was spotted.

He might not be out here. He could be in a complete opposite direction. Liam might not even want to fight for her after she didn't fight for him.

After what happened to him. She had her chance to go with him then, but she hadn't.

Another howl, and Jolie's body was getting weak from all the running she'd been doing already. Her heart slammed hot and heavy against her ribs, as though trying to break out. Her lungs were hot and dry, and so was her mouth.

She needed rest. She needed to find a place to hide, but out here there was nothing. She was bleeding and her scent was going to be stronger. Even if she did manage to find a hiding place, her scent was something much more difficult to hide, especially with the wind against her.

The courage Jolie had summoned when she'd gathered her things and made the decision to run away was gone. It was definitely gone. This was a stupid idea. She never should have done this. She never should have run into the woods. She should have taken her chances on the road. There was a chance Dempsey wouldn't have come after her and Renzo wouldn't have wanted to bother with her if she abandoned her pack.

But running into the woods? Running towards Liam, or where she thought Liam could be.

That must have pissed off Dempsey like no one's business.

And Jolie was getting to a point where she no longer cared. She didn't care if it pissed off Dempsey. She didn't care if he wanted to mate with her, or what Renzo thought, she didn't care about any of that.

She wished she'd gone with him when he'd asked her to.

She wished she hadn't turned her back on him, because now that she needed him, why would he come forward and help her?

"Liam! Liam! I'm sorry!"

It was so stupid. Announce to the wolves behind her what she was doing out here. As if they didn't already know, but now she was confirming it.

It would just get her in more trouble when she didn't show up because he wasn't out here.

That wolf Dempsey had been hunting all this time was probably not even Liam. It was probably just some rogue that Dempsey had been paranoid about, and Jolie had put her hopes in it.

"Shit!" Jolie skidded to a halt, pushing herself away from a bear trap just as she saw it. She nudged it just enough that it snapped shut, its teeth grabbing out for her, but she avoided it, thank God, and kept on running.

Dempsey had gone far out with those traps, and she was going to get her foot caught in one if she didn't watch it. Dempsey might even leave her out here to bleed out. No, he wouldn't do that. He'd just watch her until she figured out how to get out of the trap herself before making her walk back home.

It would be the ultimate walk of shame.

But he had to be out here. Liam had to be out here. It had to be him this whole time. It wasn't just Dempsey who believed it, Jolie had believed it. If she found out she was wrong now...God, she couldn't do it. She couldn't think about it.

And the wolves were getting closer. She could hear them. They were right behind her. They would have her in their sights right about now. One good burst of speed and it would be enough to catch her, throw her off her feet, and put her on her back.

They would make her submit.

Jolie's mind raced. She couldn't avoid the panicked thoughts anymore. They were there and she was definitely screwed. A weapon! She needed a weapon. A stick wouldn't work. A rock? Maybe a big one.

Jolie wanted to cry out again. She opened her mouth, Liam's name on her lips, but she didn't have anymore air left to even say his name. She was done for. She was caught.

Jolie's rubber legs gave out on her, and she fell on her face as the wolves surrounded her.

CHAPTER 3

Jolie spotted their paws before they turned into feet. Running shoes.

Made sense. Even though the clothes didn't make a difference when a shifter was in their animal form, some thought that if you were going to go out for a run in your animal shape, then it was best to wear good running shoes before the shift. As if that was going give luck, or help with posture.

Jolie spotted Dempsey's shoes, and she groaned, pushing herself to her knees. She didn't have to pay attention to the two others who were with him, just to the one guy who had it out for her.

Dempsey reached out and touched her wolf ear.

Jolie yanked her head away, her tail waving angrily, as if she was a cat instead of a wolf.

"Get a little scared, did you?"

Jolie looked away from him. Her ears and tail came out when she was high on adrenaline, not just scared, but he liked to tease her about that. No one else in the pack could make their wolf ears and tail appear when they were otherwise in their human shape. She'd been able to do it since she was a little kid. Dempsey had always liked it, so she'd tried not to do it too much after Liam was kicked out.

Dempsey sighed. He reached out, touching the soft fur of the wolf ear on top of her head again, stroking it gently between his finger and thumb before pinching down hard.

Jolie grit her teeth. Her eyes burned. She couldn't help it. It hurt!

She glared at him, showing her teeth, and her small fangs.

Dempsey smiled at her, as if that was the thing he'd been waiting to see. "There you are. Now, it's one thing for my mate to run away from me, but it's something else entirely for me to hear you calling out that name."

"I wasn't calling for anyone—ah!" Jolie let out a sharp shriek when Dempsey didn't just pinch her ear, but also dug his fingernail into the sensitive skin. As if he was getting ready to tear out a strip of flesh.

Oh God, she really didn't want him to do that to her.

"I heard that name. You're not supposed to say that name."

Jolie absorbed the pain, felt it, acknowledged it, and then pushed it down as she showed off her fangs one more time. "You say it all the time."

Dempsey's eyes turned red. The standard alpha color. It was always a little different when those red eyes started to glow.

He was mad, and he was definitely hurting her, a lot more than he'd ever done in the past.

In a way, Jolie was glad for it. She was glad to know this was who he really was. She was glad to know that she hadn't been wrong to run away from him. Why would she ever in a million years want to be mated to a man like this? Let him hurt her, he was just proving what an unworthy asshole he was.

Dempsey's eyes continued to glow, but he cocked his head

to the side just a little, as though trying to figure out what was going on inside of Jolie's head.

"Now what do you have to smile about, I wonder?"

Jolie didn't answer that. Sweat from the pain was starting to bead on her forehead, but somehow, it was kind of funny. She was glad for this. She was glad Dempsey was such a thick moron, because then he could never really break her, even if he did take her.

Then the thin flesh of her wolf ear almost felt as if it popped where his fingernail, no, his claw had been piercing her.

And she realized he'd put a hole on her.

"Oops, now look what I did," he said, pulling his hand back. There was blood on the tips of his fingers, on the claws of his thumb and forefinger.

Jolie was definitely not smiling anymore. She lifted a shaky hand to her ear, felt the heat of it, and then was sure she didn't want to confirm what she already knew.

Well, her wolf ear had a hole in it, and her palm had a slice in it. She could handle that.

"Shit, someone give me a rag," Dempsey demanded, as if he'd made the puncture wound by complete accident.

Jolie didn't think she believed that for a second, but she was smart enough to realize that it didn't matter what she believed in that moment. She was pretty much done for.

One of the betas, Dustin, pulled a red and white rag from his back pocket. Jolie yanked her head away before Dempsey could touch her with it. "Don't even think about putting that filthy thing on my ear."

"Oh?" Dempsey looked amused again. Sometimes he liked it when she fought him on certain things. Other times, he despised it. "Why is that? You're bleeding."

"He probably blew his nose in that, or wiped his hands on

it when he changed the oil in his truck. Don't touch me with it."

Dempsey looked down at the rag with renewed interest, then handed it back to Dustin.

"Right, well, I don't see any black marks on it, but now you've got me grossed out enough that I hate that I've touched it."

Jolie wished she could make him stop touching her. The instant he wiped his hands on his jeans, they came down on her shoulders, his thumbs stroking her skin.

"You don't really want me for a mate, Dempsey," Jolie said. Her last ditch effort to make him see at least some small amount of reason. "We're not good for each other."

"We can be. I like you. I like that you push my buttons, and that you're unique, and believe it or not, I like the way you're always mouthing off to Renzo. I think you're funny."

"Even when I was mouthing off yesterday at the pack meeting?"

Once again, Dempsey didn't exactly look too happy to be reminded about something like that.

That was the thing with him. He thought her snarky personality was cute and unique when it wasn't being directed at him. Every other time, he hated it, and now Jolie knew just what lengths he was willing to go to in order to make her stop.

Dempsey seemed to come to his own conclusions just then. He closed his eyes, took a breath, and when he opened them again, he was smiling at her, as if they were friends.

He dusted off her shoulders, picking a piece of lint from her summer jacket. "Okay, so here's what we're going to do. I'm going to take you home and we're going to get you cleaned up. Next week, we'll get the mating done and over with. I won't do anything to you tonight, it'll be nice and proper, just the way it's supposed to be. Does that sound nice?"

It sounded as if he thought he was being nice. Or at least making the attempt, but it wasn't good enough because Jolie still didn't want to do this. She especially didn't want to do it with him.

"Can't you just find someone else to have your pups? Why does it have to be me?"

Jolie definitely thought that would have been the wrong thing to say, but then Dempsey didn't have the reaction she expected from him.

He didn't look angry. He just kept rubbing her shoulders, as if that was supposed to be a normal thing.

"You and I, we're going to be good together. Okay? I've known that from the moment we first met, and I've given you lots of time to come to terms with this."

"You announced it yesterday."

"You knew how I felt about you. You always knew."

She did know; that was the thing she didn't like to admit to herself.

She'd known this was coming, and yet she'd been hoping that somehow it would never get to this.

That she could just continue living in the pack as long as she wanted, going about her life, doing her chores, getting her education, and maybe even a human job, and Dempsey would never touch her.

She'd been an idiot.

Dustin spoke up. "Dempsey?"

Dempsey ignored him. He kept his eyes on Jolie, his entire focus. "You're the one for me. Trust me on that."

And yet she couldn't trust him. She wasn't hard to look at, Jolie knew that much about herself, but she wasn't the best looking in the pack either. There were others—blondes, redheads, brunettes—who knew how to wear their clothes and makeup to make them look a thousand times better than Jolie did. She didn't understand this.

"You'll learn soon enough," Dempsey promised when she didn't answer.

"Dempsey," Dustin said again, and when two of the other betas backed away from the circle they'd made around Jolie and Dempsey, that was when Jolie really sat up and took notice.

They shouldn't have been doing that. They should have been protecting their defacto leader.

Dempsey growled at the lot of them. "Hey, what the fuck do you think you're..."

Dempsey didn't finish. Jolie didn't understand why until she realized he was looking at something. His attention was somewhere else, and she had to lean to the side in order to see what it was that made the words stuck in his mouth.

Jolie almost didn't see it. When she did, she thought it was a bear, and her eyes flew wide when her brain put together what it actually was.

A wolf. A big wolf. Much bigger than Jolie would have thought him to be.

The way Dempsey talked about him, Jolie would have thought he wasn't much bigger than Dempsey was when he was in his wolf form.

He was bigger all right. He might even be bigger than Renzo was.

And the hope that had flown away from Jolie renewed deep within her chest, and she smiled, begging whoever was up there that this was actually happening. "Liam?"

The wolf lowered his head, hackles raised up high, and his black lips pulled back to reveal his many sharp teeth. The teeth of an animal that didn't want these intruders in his territory.

CHAPTER 4

Wait, was he looking at her like that? He couldn't be, but he was. Was he?

Holy shit, what if he was? Or worse, what if that *wasn't* Liam?

No, it had to be. Had to. The color of fur was the same red brown color of his hair that she remembered from so long ago. The color the earth turned when she and Liam used to dig holes out in the woods, searching for worms for fishing, and they went down too deep.

That was him. That was Liam.

He just didn't recognize her.

Jolie pushed herself to her feet. "Liam! It's me!"

The wolf lunged. Dempsey pushed her out of the way, and Liam's open mouth came down hard around his middle. Dempsey started to change even before Liam's teeth could puncture his skin, and if he hadn't changed his body, let himself get bigger, his fur coming out so he could protect himself against those fangs, it might not have forced Liam to release him, and Liam might have killed him.

He might have killed Jolie if Dempsey hadn't pushed her

out of the way, and Jolie landed on her hands, opening the wound on her hand even wider. She yelped before she rolled to her back, watching the two wolves battle it out.

Dempsey, the silver and black wolf, was definitely no match. Dustin shifted, getting in on the fight, but even he looked as if he was just there to help get Dempsey out of harm's way before Liam could kill him.

Jolie couldn't look away from it. She'd seen wolf fights before, and she'd seen a wolf fight to the death, when Renzo had killed the last alpha, and she could tell that this was exactly that. The two wolves were trying to kill each other.

And from the looks of things, Dempsey was the one on the losing team.

Holy shit. This was actually going to happen.

Dempsey was either going to get killed or majorly hurt, and if she wasn't off this wolf's territory, there was the very real chance that it would lock eyes with her and make her its next meal.

Liam or not, she was getting out of here.

"Come on!" A pair of hands grabbed her. It was Red. He yanked and pulled on her, trying to get her to run with him.

She did. She couldn't look at the wolves fighting, and she didn't want Liam to turn that rage onto her.

She ran with Red. At least she ran as fast as she could. Red had an iron tight grip on her cut hand. She felt him pulling at the skin as he dragged her along. He was already faster than she was by a long shot, and if he was terrified, and more than eager to get the hell out of here, then she didn't have much to hope for either.

"Hurry up!" Red shouted back at her, damn near yanking her arm right off as he pulled her through the trees.

She was trying, but she'd been tired when Dempsey had caught up to her. Even with the adrenaline rush pulling her through, it was almost too much to handle. Her legs were weak and watery again. The way Red yanked her along didn't help since she could never catch her footing.

"R-Red, slow down," she puffed.

She definitely hadn't been in the great shape she used to think she'd been in, and she was dying for the last of the water she kept in her purse.

Red didn't slow down, and his grip on her hand burned to something so utterly painful she could hardly stand it. He was going to rip a good chunk of skin right off her hand and, even with the danger right behind her, she still felt it and it hurt!

Her foot caught. On what, she had no idea. The only thing she knew was the pain in her hand as her palm was yanked out of Red's grip, and the sensation of going down hard on her knees.

Jolie cradled her hand, trying to get up. Red turned back for her. "Come on!"

He stopped short, his eyes flying wide at something behind her, and Jolie didn't have to turn around to know what it was that had him frozen.

She trembled, a puff of air escaping her lungs, and in that moment, she didn't care about the pain in her hand or the weakness in her legs. She just didn't want to be left behind to be eaten.

"Please," she said.

Red looked down at her, and at the large creature behind her. Jolie could feel the warmth of its breath now as it closed in.

Red shook his head. "I'm sorry."

He turned and ran.

And a selfish part of Jolie honestly hoped that the wolf behind her would give chase after fleeing prey, instead of deciding to eat her.

The wolf didn't chase. It stayed behind her, breathing heavily, hotly, against her back.

A soft, mousey noise escaped her throat when she felt the cold touch of a nose against the back of her neck through her hair. The creature sniffed deeply, once, and then twice, before the sniffing became almost intense as that nose travelled around her clothes, down her back, butt, tail, and legs.

Jolie couldn't stop shivering. Every muscle in her body wound up tight and cramped as she waited for the pain of the first bite.

It was coming. Any second now, she was going to feel it and then she would be dead. She shouldn't have left. She should have found some other way of getting out of the mating. Anything was better than this.

The nose nudged her. Jolie didn't move. It nudged her again. She still didn't move.

Was he trying to get her to run? So he could chase her down? It had its opportunity to do that with Red and it turned it down. Why decide to chase her now?

Then she felt it, the soft growl, and the sensation of teeth clamping down against the collar of her jacket, pulling her up, to her feet. No, *off* of her feet.

Jolie let out a tiny shriek, then clapped her hands over her mouth, ignoring the sudden fire in her palm when she did that.

If Liam was carting her off, then the last thing she wanted was for him to mistake her for wounded prey, even though that was technically what she was.

He might let her go. If he thought she wasn't worth it, or if she peed her pants, this part of Liam that was taken over by the wild side and instinct would think her to be not worth it.

As much as she wanted to pee her pants in that moment, Jolie had used the bushes not long before being caught by Dempsey, and there was nothing left inside her. If there had, her bladder would have gone the instant she felt that nose touch the back of her neck.

    So stupid. This enormous wolf was carting her off to she didn't even know where, and all she could think about was how much she wished she could pee her pants. Knowing she was about to die apparently made her think strange thoughts.

CHAPTER 5

Eventually, the wolf started to run with her, which did not feel good in the least. Jolie cringed and cried out every time the enormous creature neatly hopped over a fallen tree, or when it picked up the pace to a happy trot.

It wasn't as if the wolf was taking a nice, easy path either. It went through the trees, shrubs, and thorny bushes. Jolie had to lift her hands on more than one occasion to keep herself from getting scratched up, all the while keeping her bleeding hand closed.

It left her with scratched up fingers, but at least nothing else was pulling at the wound she already had.

Her jacket was starting to choke her. She'd tried to loosen it, but the way the wolf bit down on the material without biting through it brought her arms back high. It made it difficult to shield her face, never mind getting the zipper and buttons down.

She felt as if she was being choked, and the wolf had been running with her for long enough that she had to pee again.

She didn't let loose, however. She was going to save that in case she needed it, a last resort. Being carried for so long also left her feeling decidedly less terrified than she'd been when the wolf turned Dempsey and Dustin into wolf meat.

It was possible that she was starting to not care so much because she was just eager for the ride to be over with, or she'd become desensitized to the scent of Dempsey's blood after so long of inhaling it within that heated breath.

At least she wasn't cold anymore.

Jolie actually started to fall asleep. She tried to fight it, tried to keep her heavy eyes open, but even with the fear of death, and the intense discomfort from this way of travelling, she couldn't do it.

When she opened her eyes again, she was horizontal, even though they were still moving.

No. They weren't moving. Nothing around them was moving so that meant she wasn't moving. She just thought she was because that up and down motion she'd been stuck with for so long had left her disoriented.

And then it hit her, she wasn't moving. That was kind of important after everything that had happened.

With a hiss, she sat up straight, eyes wide, trying to get her bearings and look around at what was happening, or where she was.

It was difficult. Long shadows were everywhere, and the space around her wouldn't stop moving, tilting and turning.

She was dizzy, and her palm...it was bandaged, and bandaged well. She'd wondered why her hand felt so stiff, but it had been cleaned and taken care of.

She was also warm, and not because of wolf breath.

There was a thick animal pelt over her body, blanketing her, and a hot fire. It was crackling, just over there, lighting up the dark space she inhabited. She almost wouldn't have noticed it had it not been for that ongoing white noise from just over there.

Water. The sounds she heard were the whoosh of water and

the crackle of fire, and someone was kneeling in front of the fire. She hadn't seen him at first, not with the way her vision was still playing tricks on her, and the long shadows that flickered everywhere, but when she narrowed her eyes and forced her vision to unblur, that was definitely a man she was looking at.

"Hello?"

He raised his head at the sound of her voice. Long auburn hair shone in the firelight. It went halfway down his back, and he was completely naked.

Jolie didn't dare to hope, not even when he turned around to look at her and she got a look at his face.

With the fire behind him casting light to his back and the long hair that framed his shoulders, it cast awkward angles of light over his face, making him appear mean, almost as if he was a monster ready to spring.

But she could still see him. Jolie could still make out the boy she'd known when she was thirteen. She'd followed him around everywhere, slept in his house after her parents died, and ate at the same table he ate at with his mother and father.

She could almost see the way he used to smile, and if there had been any lingering doubt left in her head, it vanished with this new vision of him.

"Liam?"

At least she wouldn't have to pee her pants anymore. Jolie wanted to go to him, to touch his face, to hug him, and to kiss him and tell him she was sorry.

Even with everything she'd done to him, she knew he wouldn't want to hurt her. He wouldn't be eating her tonight, or any other night.

He was here, this was him, her Liam, and the rush of excited giddiness that sprung up inside her nearly made her explode purple puffs of sparkles and stars. That was how on top of the moon she was to see him.

"I knew it was you," she said. "I used to see a wolf prowling around the outskirts of the territory. Whenever I saw a pair of yellow eyes watching from the trees, I knew it was you, and then Dempsey always complained about you. He could never catch you."

So happy. She couldn't contain it. Her chest was about to burst with the amount of happiness that rushed through her. She didn't know what to do with this sudden rush of energy she had.

Jolie released a broken laugh. "Will you say something?"

Liam continued to look at her, his eyes hard, as if he was observing her. Studying her.

The smile slowly melted from Jolie's mouth, the realization that this might not be the happy reunion she'd originally thought hitting her, and it hit hard.

"Liam?"

As he looked at her, it allowed her to study him back. She saw a few things on him that were different from what she'd originally thought she'd seen. Rough details around the edges that were hard to ignore now that her joyous haze faded away.

At first she saw the face of the boy who was her best friend. She saw the ghosts of his old smiles as he stared at her, but now that she really forced herself to stare at him, she could see the hard press of his mouth, the scar that ran down the corner of his bottom lip and across his forehead at a crooked, barely there angle.

He looked older, harder, and not just because he was older. No, it was in his eyes and in his flesh. The world hadn't been kind to him since he'd been thrown out of the pack all those years ago.

She wasn't sure why that was a shock, or why it made her so sad only now. She'd known this before making the decision to run to him, and yet…now that she could see him standing naked in front of her…

"Liam? Do you recognize me? Do you…do you understand what I'm saying?"

His eyes narrowed, as though insulted. "Of course I understand what you're saying."

The words that came from his mouth made her sigh with relief. "You can understand me."

"I've been living on my own since I was fourteen, not four," he muttered, turning his back on her, giving his attention back to the fire. He stoked it. He was cooking something.

That shocked her.

"What are you doing here?"

Jolie swallowed. Now that she was awake and here, she no longer had that rush of excitement. Now there was something that was a little close to fear. Not necessarily of him, but of the potential rejection.

He couldn't reject her. She repeated that at least three times in her head before speaking. "I came to ask for your help, but you already took care of Dempsey."

Liam snorted, then muttered, "He ran away, coward."

"So…he's alive?" Another shocking revelation. The way Liam had been fighting with Dempsey made her think he wouldn't have let the man live.

"I should have killed him, but the other one was taking you away." Liam looked back at her. "Was that Red?"

Jolie wet her bottom lip, and she nodded. "Yeah, that was Red."

"Oh." Liam turned back to the fire, sighing, shaking his head. "I thought…somehow…."

Jolie waited for him to finish. When he said nothing else, she prompted him. "What did you think?"

Liam shook his head, briefly glancing back at her. "Nothing. What are you doing all the way out here anyway?"

"I came for your help."

He kept his eyes on the fire. "You said that. What do you want?"

She couldn't remember him being this short with her before. He'd always been something of a mischief maker, always looking for the next bit of fun to have, but never so gruff.

At least not with her.

She supposed that accidentally killing his step father, the man who had been abusing his mother after the death of his father, and then being kicked out of the pack might have that sort of an impact. She was going to have to tread carefully. The life she'd lived after he left was probably a cakewalk in comparison. He probably thought all the problems she'd faced over the years were a joke.

"Well?"

Even though he wouldn't look at her, Jolie couldn't look away from him. Now that she was here, the only thing she wanted to do was to go to him, put her arms around him, and comfort him, make up for all the nights when she hadn't been there.

That wouldn't be a welcome gesture at this point.

"It's hard to explain. You might get mad at me if I told you," she said.

Chicken. She was a total chicken.

Liam let out a gruff noise. He stabbed at the flames with his stick one more time.

Jolie glanced around the cave, knowing now that it was probably his home. She realized that was indeed the case when she spotted a crate over in the far corner, and, to her shock, a few books on top of it, and even some clothes. So he could apparently get dressed when he needed to. He wasn't entirely wild. That was good to know.

"Renzo, he's still the alpha, did you know that?"

She almost wished there was a way to warn him she would even say that name, considering Renzo had killed Liam's father in a fight for dominance of the pack.

And then banished Liam after the mess with his mother.

Liam growled, stabbing is stick harder into the fire, making sparks fly. "Yes. Hard not to smell that prick whenever Dempsey comes looking for a fight."

Jolie swallowed hard. "He gave me to Dempsey."

Liam rounded on her. "He *what?*"

Jolie wet her lips, swallowing hard, torn between pleasure that he would care and worry over the dark look on his face, and the red in his eyes.

"Tell me what he did."

"He didn't do anything. Yet. Dempsey wanted me to mate with him. I guess he'd been asking Renzo for a while, and Renzo finally said yes. I was to...be his mate."

Once again, Liam stared at her, his eyes giving almost nothing away, but he was clearly searching. "That's why you wanted me?" he said, a soft growl underlining his voice. "All this time, and you come back to me because you wanted me to kill Dempsey for you?"

"*No!*" Christ, he couldn't have been more wrong if he tried. "It wasn't like that. I don't want you to kill anyone. I don't want anyone to die."

"And yet you came running into the woods to get me to...do what? What else would you want me to do after you turned your back on me?"

"I was thirteen!" Jolie shouted. "You'd been kicked out of the pack, it was scary enough. I had no idea what was going to happen."

Liam shot to his feet. "I would have taken care of you!"

"You haven't even taken care of yourself."

She regretted those words the instant they were out of her mouth. The look on Liam's face, the betrayal, the anger, and the disgust as she judged the home he'd made for himself, was evident.

"I've survived here just fine on my own. I could have gone anywhere, but I stayed."

She had a feeling why, but she needed him to say it out loud. Her heart pounded. "And why was that?"

Say it. Please, say it.

He didn't answer. He just turned his back to the fire. He turned the meat that had been skewered there before it could burn too much. Jolie was definitely distracting him.

"So did you want me to kill Dempsey or just beat the shit out of him? I did one of those two things already, so I hope that's enough to keep you happy."

"I didn't want you to kill him, but maybe help me keep him off my back. Which I guess you did. Thank you for that, and for not killing him."

Liam snorted. He poked at the meat on the skewer, apparently deciding that was enough, and then pulled the metal rod off the two prongs that kept it just the right amount of distance above the fire.

He turned towards her, handing her the cooked meat. "Here, eat this. Don't touch the metal in the middle just yet, you'll burn yourself."

She took the end of the metal rod he offered, staring down at the sizzling meat, and then up at him. It was a big deal for an alpha to offer food to someone else. It was an even bigger deal when he cooked it first.

Her happiness and hope rekindled. In that moment, she knew she'd made the right choice.

"I always wondered why you stuck around," she said.

"Uh huh," Liam said, sitting in front of her, crossing his

legs. Jolie had to do her absolute best to keep her eyes above his waist, to not stare at his nudity, the scars on his body, or let herself get carried away with how perfect his body was, despite those scars.

Down, girl—they weren't there yet.

"Why did you think I never left?"

"Because of me?" It wasn't entirely meant to come out as a question, but she wanted to ease him into this as gently as possible.

She hoped it was true. She'd always thought about it, definitely suspected it over the years, but she'd been so young at the time, and he had been, too.

The way Liam's scarred mouth turned up at the corner didn't exactly give her the confidence she was searching for. "You thought I stayed out here, poaching on pack territory all this time, because of you?"

"You asked me to leave with you. You came back for me that night and asked at the window."

The smile melted off Liam's face. He growled at her. Apparently, he didn't like the memory of when she'd turned him down and decided to stay.

"Like you said, you could have gone anywhere."

"I was a child."

"I know," Jolie said. "And instead of going to a shelter, or the police, of getting put into a foster home or of even trying to find a job, you stayed out here. You learned how to take care of yourself, and for the first couple of years, I would see you sometimes. You can't tell me that wasn't you."

He was always so far away to the point she could hardly be sure there had been anyone watching her at all, but Jolie had been sure there had been someone out there. She'd seen his eyes glowing in the distance from time to time, and it used to make her happy, but then, as she got older, it made her sad, because she knew what it meant.

It meant that he was still fending for himself, living out in the wild, and possibly getting lost to the instinct of his wolf —going wild.

Liam continued to growl at her, to glare at her. It was an obvious warning, but one she couldn't refuse.

"You stayed for me, because maybe you didn't realize it at first, but I was more than just your best friend."

"*Shut up.*"

"I was your mate. Your true mate. I still am."

Liam grabbed her by the throat.

CHAPTER 6

He slammed her back down on the pelts she'd been sleeping on, his body coming on top of hers. At first his grip around her neck was rough, tight enough to keep any air from getting inside, but then, immediately, he released her, his eyes widening as he pushed himself to his feet and walked away.

Jolie panted and puffed for breath. She blinked up at the ceiling of the cave above her, and then turned her head to look at where Liam was going. He walked through the curtain of water that kept the cave hidden away, and then was gone.

Jolie pushed herself back into a sitting position. She kept watching, waiting for him to come back, to tell her if she was wrong.

Or right.

But she was right. She'd known it deep within herself for years. There was no way in hell she was wrong about this.

And he knew it, too.

She got to her feet. Her shoes and socks had been sitting

neatly beside her. Jolie grabbed them, put them on, and then rushed to the flow of water.

The waterfall didn't flow immediately against the rock. It branched off, creating a thin pathway she could follow along the side of the cave entrance, allowing her to get out without soaking herself.

It explained how Liam had managed to get her into his hideaway without getting her or her clothes wet.

She followed it out. She didn't know this waterfall, but the flow of water was strong. There could be rapids just a little farther downstream for the water to be this powerful right here.

When she stepped out from behind the waterfall, the light confused her. She thought for a split second it might have been sundown, but no, the sun was on the wrong side of the sky.

It was dawn.

Liam was in the water up to his thighs. He stared down into the stream, his hands out, claws where his normal fingernails were supposed to be at the ready.

Was he catching a fish? Did salmon come up this way?

He didn't seem to notice the cold of the water he was in, and Jolie could see no signs of any goosebumps forming on his skin.

She hadn't been in the water, but walking behind the waterfall had been enough to let her feel the overall cold of it. It was almost enough to make her want to go back to his nice and cozy fire.

She didn't. Jolie walked along the side of the river, getting up behind him, watching how silent and steady he was as he hunted his new prey.

She had been thinking about this for years. Jolie had dreamed about the things she would say to him if she ever saw him again. Now she was here, and she was about to completely mess this up because she had to push things.

Renzo liked to bitch about how she let her mouth get the better of her.

So Jolie stayed silent. For now. She watched Liam work. When she'd known him, he'd shown promise for becoming an alpha, but he didn't have the discipline, and after his father had died…things had just been worse. He'd been angry. Then his stepfather had come into the picture and everything went to shit.

To see him right now, even though he'd just lost his temper with her, to be standing there patiently waiting for his catch to come to him…it was an amazing sight.

There were more scars on his back. They were deeper than the ones on his mouth and face. A few were scattered about his shoulders. One looked like a stab wound instead of claw marks.

Jolie wasn't sure if she should be worried about that.

Finally, after a long silence, Liam's hands moved, coming together tightly beneath the water, grabbing his prey, lifting it above the water.

The fish flicked its tail back and forth in a wild, desperate attempt to dislodge itself and be free, but Liam's claws were dug into the side of the belly, locking it in place, dooming it.

It was a big one, too. Maybe not enough to fill the belly of an alpha, but it was something.

Liam turned around, his catch in hand. Their eyes met.

Jolie smiled at him. "Good catch."

He turned his gaze away. "For you."

Jolie blinked at that. "Me?" She didn't understand. "You gave me something."

The meat on a stick he'd been cooking. Rabbit or squirrel, she couldn't tell.

"And it was dropped in on the floor of the cave. It's dirty there."

Liam still wouldn't look at her as he left the water, holding his catch, which was no longer struggling quite so hard to escape.

He walked right by her, still avoiding her eyes, but she was so intensely aware of him, of his body and size, that it wasn't possible he couldn't be feeling the same way about her.

She followed after him. "Are you angry because I didn't go with you? That's it, right?"

Liam sighed. "I'm sorry I grabbed your throat. I didn't mean to do that."

"Was it because you spent so much time out here? On your own?"

"Please come inside," Liam said, his voice hardly sounding patient about the whole thing. "It's safer inside and I can cook a new meal for you."

Okay, so staying silent wasn't going to work. "I'm your mate, Liam, and I just told you that after years of being apart, and after telling you about Dempsey. I'm sorry. I should have tried to come find you sooner."

"Like you said, you were a child."

"And so were you, and you were alone when I should have been there with you." That last part of her sentence came out choked. Jolie couldn't help it. Her heart ached to think about what he'd gone through when she wasn't there.

It wasn't as if she would have been a good hunter, or a decent protector. If anything, he would have been doing the majority of that, but at the same time, she could have been there for him. She could have comforted him, made sure he wasn't cold in the night when he tried to go to sleep out in the open.

How many close calls did he have? How many animals

had he fought with and injured himself, only to have to take care of himself with no one there to help him?

Those were the best case scenarios. Despite how well he'd taken care of Dempsey and Dustin, then scared off Red, she had no doubt in her mind that some of those scars on his body had come from Dempsey.

As if to make sure, she glanced down as his ankles. There were definitely scars down there that looked as though they had come from the traps Dempsey had set out.

One more thing for him to have dealt with on his own.

If she had been there, maybe it wouldn't have been so bad, and she wouldn't be in this position. She wouldn't be looking at her best friend as if he was a stranger to her when he definitely wasn't.

"I'm sorry."

"Stop apologizing."

"I can't help it. I need to, because you're right to be mad. I didn't come with you, and then I only tried to find you after I needed something from you. That's not right."

And she felt like a complete asshole for it. She'd known it was a selfish thing to do when she'd gathered up a few things and took off, but now that she was here and in front of him, it was different.

So much needed to be said. She had so many things she wanted to tell him, that she had to tell him.

Liam just sighed. "Get inside and we'll talk. After I feed you."

This was clearly the best she was going to get, and Jolie figured she might as well take it.

"Does this mean you believe me? About being mated?"

Liam's eyes changed to a bright shade of red, though he looked away from her again, his chest heaving as he inhaled and exhaled heavily. "You shouldn't tempt me. You said it yourself, my wolf is wilder than most."

"That doesn't matter."

"It matters to me," Liam snapped, his hard gaze returning to her in another harsh glare.

Jolie bit her lips together. Suddenly feeling cold, she brought her hands up to cover her arms.

She hadn't felt this small since...

Since Liam had been forced out of the pack.

"I know I wasn't there for you before, but I'm here now."

"And you've seen exactly what I can offer you," Liam said. "A cave dwelling and an angry wolf powerful enough to snap you in half if I'm not careful."

Jolie shook her head. "I don't think you would do that to me."

Liam shook his head, muttering under his breath.

Jolie didn't catch much of what he'd just said, but she definitely heard the word *stubborn* uttered in there.

They practically had a stand-off. Jolie could hardly look at him, and he seemed to be refusing to look at her.

When he did, it was only briefly, and he nodded in her direction before looking away again. "Your ears and tail came out again."

Force of habit had Jolie reaching up, feeling for herself that her ears were there. She had to put all her strength and willpower into keeping her tail from tucking between her legs, though she did smile. "Yeah, that still happens."

Liam smiled at that, shaking his head. "Come inside and eat or don't. It doesn't matter to me."

He turned his back on her for real this time, walking back into his cave, not bothering with taking the slightly longer way that would have kept him from getting wet.

Since he already was wet, she supposed it didn't matter.

But one thing did matter, and that was his reaction towards her.

He wasn't going to admit it, that was fine. Jolie wasn't

giving up, because she *could* feel this, and she knew he could feel it, too.

Maybe it was something about living in the wild for so long, but while Liam wasn't making an issue out of it, Jolie had been able to see the reaction of his groin when he got out of the water.

The cold water hadn't been enough to stop his body from reacting and an erection from forming, or to shrink him down if the size of him was anything to go by.

Yes. She was definitely right about this. They were mated, and Jolie was going to be with her true mate or no one else.

CHAPTER 7

"I've got money."

Liam froze, and then turned to face her, his eyes narrowed suspiciously.

And with insult.

"So?"

Jolie swallowed hard. "It's not a lot, but it's enough that we can get a room somewhere for a couple of days, hide out if we want to. We could rent a car, or get a train ticket, anything to get far away from here." He was shaking his head. That wasn't a good sign. Jolie pressed on. "I can get a job. There's enough to give us the first and last month's rent for an apartment. We can have a normal life away from this place."

"You would abandon your pack?"

She didn't understand. "Renzo wants to give me to Dempsey. Did you forget about that?"

"Of course not. It's why you came to me in the first place."

Jolie cringed. "I told you I was sorry for that. Doesn't that count for anything? We were children."

Liam said nothing. He let out one of his claws. It was

sharp enough that, as he crouched down, he was able to neatly clean out the guts of the fish and stick it over the fire for cooking.

Jolie didn't like that he'd been living this way for so long.

"I want to help you, too," she said. "We can be normal people again."

"Shifters are never normal. Your ears and tail are sticking out right now. That's not normal."

Jolie reached out to touch the soft fur of her wolf ear. She dropped her hand. Somehow, she'd always thought that only Renzo would be able to make her feel so small. She hadn't expected this from Liam, but then again, it wasn't as if they actually knew each other anymore.

"Is it because you don't want a woman taking care of you?"

"Don't you dare try and make this out to be about that." Liam shot to his feet. He rounded on her, his eyes blazing with anger. "This has nothing to do with you being a woman, and everything to do with me. That pack is still my home. You might want to leave it, but I can't."

"I thought you couldn't leave it because of me?"

The words came out of her before she could stop them. Jolie slammed her mouth shut, wishing she could take them back, knowing what she'd just revealed to this man.

And Liam growled at her. "That wasn't the only reason, but I'm wild now. I barely have a grade seven education. I'm not comfortable wearing clothes anymore so I stay in my wolf shape, or like this. How do you ever expect me to get a normal human job? Would you think I was so romantically tragic when I can't even keep work flipping burgers to pay for your small apartment?"

"So then if it's not about you being taken care of by a woman, it's about your pride?"

She didn't say it judgmentally. There was no way she

could judge him for that. He was an alpha, after all. Their pride was a thing of legends.

"It's not about my pride and it's not about being taken care of by a woman, it's about being taken care of by you."

Jolie fell back a step, as if he'd just shoved her. Her heart thundered beneath her ribs, painful, swelling and aching, and she could hardly breathe over the lump in her throat.

And she wanted to cry. "Do you really hate me that much?"

The scowl melted away from Liam's brow. His eyes no longer held that blazing hatred she'd seen there just a moment before. Now there was something else, a clarity Jolie could hardly appreciate, especially when she heard Dempsey's voice calling out her and Liam's name from beyond the waterfall.

"Liam! Jolie! I know you're both in there so you might as well come out."

Liam lifted his gaze towards the waterfall, as if he expected someone to come rushing in at any moment. His lips pulled back, revealing teeth that were less than human as his nostrils flared.

He charged forward two steps before Jolie grabbed him by the arm. "No, don't."

"He'll die this time."

"He probably has a gun pointed at the entrance and will shoot you the second he sees you coming out. Is there another way out of here?"

Liam looked down at her, and then back towards the source of the noise. He growled again, low in his throat, and his strong hand took a painful grip on Jolie's arm. He yanked her towards the back of the cave, behind the fire.

It almost looked as though Liam had carved out a neat space for himself at some point. The uneven patches and rough scratch mark made her shiver to think of him doing it with his claws, but at a certain point, the ceiling of the cave sank down lower and lower. Liam had to duck his head before Jolie did, and then he was crouching and pointing to a small space that looked like a claustrophobe's worst nightmare.

"I can wiggle through there if I try hard enough. You should be able to squeeze your way through."

"Where does it go?" Jolie had never in her life thought of herself as being afraid of small and dark spaces, but now that she was faced with the probability of pushing her body between the rock and hard packed earth that could crush her if it caved in...she didn't want to go in there.

"In about fifty feet, it will take you around to hills, away from where they can see you, and if the wind is right, they shouldn't be able to smell you down there either, not before it's too late."

Dempsey screamed for them again. "Don't play stupid with me. I know you're both in there, you might as well come out now."

"You're coming with me, right?" Jolie asked. "What if I get stuck?"

And what if Liam was just getting rid of her so he could safely charge out there and attack?

Something that would likely get him killed.

Liam's lips thinned, as if he really did not want to be having this conversation. "I'll be right behind you."

Jolie blinked, and her gut clenched.

Maybe it was the fact that she was connected to him as a real, natural mate, or it could have been their history together. It could have been any number of things, but she just knew he was lying to her.

"Go," he said, pointing to the little crevice she was expected to crawl through.

Jolie looked down at it, and then at him. And she was pissed beyond belief.

So, despite that anger, or possibly because of it, she grabbed tightly to Liam's ears and yanked his face forward, crushing his mouth to hers.

The widening of his eyes was a good thing. It meant she'd caught him off guard. Jolie had almost started to believe that wouldn't be possible, but now that it was, she was rejuvenated. Jolie could do this, and she pulled back with a smile.

"If we're going to be doing this, you're never allowed to lie to me again."

Liam blinked, his eyes huge, dilated, and maybe he didn't catch a word she'd said, but that was all right, and before he could stop her, Jolie rushed to the edge of the water fall.

Liam's hands reached out for her, trying to grab her, but she stayed out of his reach.

"Dempsey! I'm coming out."

CHAPTER 8

It was a risk, a huge risk, but Jolie needed to take it if it kept Liam from going out there. From getting shot.

She hot-footed it as quickly as she could along the wall of the waterfall, coming out behind it on the rock.

Liam didn't follow her, which was good. All eyes were currently on her. She even felt Liam's stare as he watched her through the water. If he came any closer, he would be seen.

His stare was the hottest against the back of her neck, but that was fine. As long as he stayed where he was, he would be fine. He could be an alpha, and a huge wolf on top of that, but shifters were not immune to bullet holes.

"Hello, Jolie," Dempsey said. His hands were pressed firmly on his hips, and his lower lip was split and red, though not bleeding.

It looked as if it had been not too long ago, and a lot. The fact that both of his eyes were also black added up to how much he looked like complete shit. That was a hard thing for a guy who was normally good-looking to do.

"Hi, Dempsey." Red was back with him, and so was Dustin, but Carl was there as well as Patrick. None of them had guns pointed at her, or in hand, but she could see the holsters. "Are those really necessary?"

"Maybe." Dempsey shrugged. "Depends on where he is."

Jolie took two steps down the damp rock, keeping herself away from the water. She didn't step onto the grass, however.

It was as if she was still safe on the rock, as though stepping on the grass was a form of surrender, which was not what she was doing.

"Well," Dempsey asked, impatiently. "He in there with you?"

She shrugged. "Go inside and see for yourself."

Dempsey managed to keep his expression fairly neutral, considering he looked very much as if he'd been having a bad couple of days. "Now you know that is hardly fair," he said. "Come on, I came all the way out here to get you, to save you, really, and you're gonna be all sarcastic?" Dempsey shook his head. "You know, I usually think it's cute and all, but when we get mated, that shit's gonna stop."

Jolie blinked wide. She was honest to God shocked that he would still keep it in his head that there could be even a remote chance of them being together.

"I thought I made myself clear when I left," Jolie said.

"You're special," Dempsey replied. "We have one fight, and you think that's it? Come on, if we're gonna make this work, you and I are gonna need to put in some more effort than that. I can even get us a marriage counselor if you like. Huh? Does that sound good? Get all your feelings out in the open with a nice psychiatrist. I'll find one that's a shifter, too, so you can say whatever the hell you want, and I can get to work on providing like a good alpha."

She couldn't stop looking at him as if he was crazy. He

wasn't, he was perfectly sane. She knew that much about him, but the fact that he wasn't letting this go suggested there was definitely something unhinged with him.

"You don't look impressed. Does she look impressed?" Dempsey looked to Carl as he pointed to Jolie.

Carl shrugged. "Not really."

He looked so uncomfortable to be asked that. None of the men with Dempsey looked happy to be where they were. They shifted from foot to foot, mouths pressed in firm lines, as if they were trying to hold back some unpleasant gas.

Jolie felt the pity in their eyes, and as much as she didn't like it, she understood it.

These were good shifters, but good men did bad things when they had to, and shifters in a pack were no different.

Jolie was going to have to work hard to make sure Dempsey couldn't take her. Not just for herself, but she knew Red. She knew Dustin, and Carl, and Patrick. She didn't want them to feel guilty for the rest of their lives that they'd brought her in against her will, so her mission was to just make sure she wasn't caught.

"What if I said I wanted a marriage counselor, but didn't want to marry you or mate with you until after I was two hundred and ten percent satisfied with the way things were going?"

She hoped Liam didn't hear that, and if he did, she also hoped he would understand why she'd said what she had.

"Two hundred?" Dempsey asked, his eyes popping wide.

"And ten," Jolie added. "A year, possibly two years of therapy, and I don't believe in sex before mating or marriage, so you would have to keep your hands to yourself, and I would need an escort if you wanted to take me out."

"Bullshit!" Dempsey said, half shouting and half laughing the words. "How do I know you didn't—"

He cut himself off, lowering his hand just as he pointed at

the waterfall. He looked away from her and backed off, and she could see the clench in his cheek right before he smiled.

"You know what? I'm not going to let myself get worked up over that. The point is that I'm here now, you're here now, and as soon as we take care of that asshole, we can wipe the slate clean. We'll make it as if this whole thing never happened. That's a good thing, right?"

He seemed to be waiting for an answer. Another shock since something like that came off as being a rhetorical question.

"I honestly don't know what you want me to say to that."

Dempsey clapped his hands together, a smile on his face. "That's better than a full on no."

"You haven't been listening to my nos."

"Whatever, someone go help my princess down from those slippery rocks and check behind that waterfall. I smell food cooking and one asshole wolf that needs to be put in his place. Get him out here, or just shoot him. If you think he's about to attack you, shoot him."

"No, wait, Dempsey." Jolie struggled to quickly get down from the slippery, rocky ledge. It was only about a foot or so off the ground and she didn't need the help. Or for anyone to put their hands on her, but she wanted them searching the waterfall even less.

Red bypassed her by walking through the water, getting ready to go through the falls.

"Red, come on," Jolie begged.

He barely glanced at her before pushing through the water.

Jolie turned back to Dempsey. "He's not here anyway. He left."

"Then why are you so worried about having your hidey hole checked?"

Jolie wished she was a beta. She wanted to leap on him

and claw his eyes out so badly, but she wasn't strong enough for that, and it didn't matter how much Dempsey liked her, or thought he liked her, she doubted he would be willing to put up with her attacking him.

Patrick stepped forward, reaching out and taking her by the elbow. His grip was tight, but not enough to hurt her.

She looked at him, and she was definitely getting tired of seeing that pitying expression on people's faces.

"Come on, this doesn't have to be so hard."

Jolie glared at him, then punched him in the stomach when she couldn't contain her rage.

The force of her fist hitting him in the gut made him cough and constrict a little, but then he was glaring down at her, and Jolie had a fist of throbbing knuckles.

"Patrick, just bring her over here. I'm sure she didn't mean it," Dempsey called.

Patrick did as he was told, yanking her along, probably a little harder than he really needed to. Jolie walked, but only because she had to.

Dempsey smiled as she approached, as if he was having his favorite toy returned to him.

"There, now this doesn't need to be hard, now does it?"

Jolie yanked her arm out of Patrick's hand, though she knew she was only able to get away because he loosened his grip and allowed it. "You know, if you really want me to be your mate, you should probably stop with talking to me like a fucking child. Makes a girl wonder what you're actually into."

Dempsey barked a laugh. "There! You see! This isn't going to break you. I'll let you get away with that one because it was a zinger, but otherwise, sweetness, you're going to have to zip it."

"But I—"

"*Shh!*"

The way he hissed it at her took Jolie aback.

Dempsey lifted a single finger, a warning for her to say nothing else.

"You can't just—"

"*Shh!*"

"I won't be—"

"Zip it!"

"Will you stop that!"

"Okay, darling, I'm going to need you to do less of this right here. See this?" He flapped his fingers and thumb together again and again, a pair of chatty lips. "Less of this, and more of this." He closed his fingers and thumb together.

Jolie clenched her hands into fists, and she didn't care if it hurt her palm.

"You see that? Less of this..." The flapping fingers. "And more of this." Closed again.

Jolie glared up at him. "I get it."

"And yet you're still talking."

She wanted to tell him that whoever was unlucky enough to mate with him, a real mating, was going to be annoyed to hell and back for having to put up with his bullshit, but she didn't want to get hissed at again.

Red came back out of the falls, shaking the water from his red hair. "There's no one in there. Just a campfire and some clothes. He's been in there before. I think he *lives* here."

"It seriously took you that long to get in there, have a quick look and sniff before you decided to come out here and tell me that? What were you doing, marking your territory?"

Red glanced away just long enough for it to be clear he was embarrassed.

Jolie struggled to hold back a laugh. "Are you serious? You were marking your territory? Can't you control yourself?"

Betas were known to mark their territory for the alphas

they worked for when there was a rogue alpha nearby. Supposedly, it was instinct. Jolie wasn't so sure about that. She always thought it was a convenient excuse for the men to whip it out and take a pee outdoors whenever the urge hit them. Mostly she thought this because, as far as she knew, she'd never seen a female beta squatting down against a tree or building to mark her territory.

That was insane, and gross enough, but the sudden heat in Jolie's gut pulled her attention to something else. She looked to the side, into the trees.

She saw nothing. Not really. There were the trees and bushes, the sounds of crickets and chirping birds, and then the whooshing noise of the waterfall itself, but there was also…something.

Yet she spotted no shadows between the bushes and branches. She caught no sight of movement that couldn't be explained by the subtle breeze in the area, and yet there *was* something out there.

She knew what it was. Even though she couldn't see him, he was there, and he was doing what she'd given him the chance to do.

Good.

Dempsey hardly seemed to notice. He was too busy being impatient and cranky. "Christ, whatever, can we just get out of here already? I'll get some more betas out here to watch the place. If it wasn't under a waterfall, I'd burn it."

Jolie couldn't believe it. "Dempsey, you can't be serious. You brought two other people with you today that weren't here when Liam thrashed you. Do you really think a couple of betas around here are going to keep him from coming back?"

"Some of these might," Dempsey replied, lifting his shirt and pulling out the gun for her to get a proper look at it.

Jolie shook her head. "Dempsey, I'm not going with you, and I'm pretty sure you would need to sneak up on him for the guns to be worth it."

Or for Liam to get stupid and think he could just charge out there and slash everyone to pieces when they had guns instead of playing it smart.

Dempsey smiled at her, his head tilting to the side just a little. "Sweetie, I thought we just agreed that you were coming with me? Okay? Best to not confuse me right now, I'm not in the best of moods."

"Yeah, I can see that, but I'm still not coming with you."

Dempsey's head fell back. He heaved the heaviest sigh she'd ever heard from him. "Okay, why? What do you need now?"

"Nothing you can give me."

She could slowly see the purple color rising up his neck. She was almost proud of him for trying to contain his usual rage, but at the same time, it was easy to remember that this was the guy who was trying to force her hand into a mating, so then that pride quickly vanished.

"You are so fucking...you know what? Forget this. I'm your alpha so I'll just take you home."

Jolie backed up as he walked towards her. "Don't touch me, Dempsey."

"Uh huh, we can talk about it when we get home. I'm sure after a couple of years of wedded bliss you'll find it in your hard, cold heart to forgive me."

He reached out, snatching her by the arm.

Jolie tried to pull back. "Hey!"

His grip tightened, and Jolie found herself walking into the water, pulling him with her, and he was clearly getting pissed off.

"Come here, stop making this so hard on us."

"There is no us, you idiot!"

Jolie yanked on her wrists, getting one of them free, and then pulling back hard before slapping him in the face with all the force she had in her body.

Her palm cracked perfectly against his cheek, and that dark purple color of rage slid the rest of the way up his face, making his transformation into a grape complete.

He smacked her back. It didn't hurt right away, though she felt it. Her body flew back. The only thing that kept her from going right in the water was the fact that he still had her by her arms and kept her on her feet.

Liam was taking his sweet time getting here, that was for sure.

"Now I promise," Dempsey started "that I am not the sort of alpha who hits an omega, not often, and I don't like doing it when it does have to happen, so that hurt me more than it did you."

"Ow, I doubt it," Jolie moaned, lifting her hand to her jaw. She definitely felt as if something as a little off center. She hoped that was just the ache she felt and not something that was actually misplaced in her jaw.

"Okay, well, whatever. We'll put some ice on that when we get home. For now, just stop fighting me—"

The sound of Red's horrified scream pulled Dempsey's attention away from Jolie and towards the man who worked for him.

Jolie had to look, too. She couldn't not look towards the source of that hideous shrieking sound.

Red trembled on the tips of his toes, held there in place by the four long claws that had punched right through his shoulder. The muscles in his face spasmed, and with the way his mouth was dropped open, it was clear he was still trying to scream, but just couldn't get the sound out. Not through the pain.

"Shit," Dempsey muttered.

Jolie acted fast, pulling his gun out of his holster and pointing it at his face before he could use her as a human shield. "Get back, right now."

CHAPTER 9

Dempsey stumbled away about three steps, his hands lifted only a little, and though he was clearly confused, a set of emotions played across his face that had Jolie wondering which one he would settle on. Amusement, rage, or just more confusion.

"Do you even know how to use that thing?" he finally asked, apparently settling on amusement.

Jolie wiped the annoying little smirk off his face when she pulled back on the hammer of the gun. The clicking noise it made created a nice sense of danger that even Dempsey couldn't ignore.

"I know how to use a gun," she said.

She was an omega. It wasn't as if she'd be able to fight properly with just her strength and claws. She barely had those to begin with.

"Liam, please don't kill Red. He's actually not a bad guy."

Liam growled. "Lot's changed since we last saw each other."

Liam wouldn't know everyone who had come to the pack since he'd left. Red was one of the people he had known, but he was right. The people he'd known as a child had grown up. People were different, and right now, to him, Red was a threat.

Jolie didn't want anyone to die if she could help it. "Just don't kill him."

Liam made another audible growling noise. "Why shouldn't I?"

Jolie really hoped he was asking that to put a sense of fear into the others. He was definitely branding a sense of fear into Red.

"Liam," Dempsey said, as if he was bored with the entire situation. "How's my not so favorite stepbrother been doing? Not so well from the looks of it."

"Doing better than your father." He held Red tight enough to make a pained whimper squeak out of the man.

Jolie was feeling sympathy pains for Red, and she forced herself to not look at either him or Liam, keeping her focus on Dempsey instead.

At the mention of his father, whom Liam had killed, fur started to sprout on Dempsey's face, as if he was fighting back a transformation.

"Yeah, I guess this shit hole you keep yourself in is marginally better than where my dad is, but then I comfort myself with the knowledge that, well, since my dad killed your mom, we're kind of even."

"Dempsey, shut the fuck up!" Jolie snapped.

That was by far the most horrible thing he could have said. She wasn't even sure why it shocked her to hear it coming out of his mouth.

"What? You're going to take his side?" Dempsey snapped, staring at Jolie as though he'd expected her to take his. "After he just made fun of my dead father, you think *he* has the high ground on anything?"

These two wolves hated each other, they always had and

would, but at least when Liam killed Dempsey's father, it was to try to defend his dying mother, whom Dempsey's father had attacked one too many times.

"He was trying to save his mother, you know that."

"Bullshit. She was already dead, and this asshole wasn't defending shit. He was getting revenge. That's different."

"And it was good when he begged me not to kill him," Liam said, stomping his foot down on Dempsey's emotionally open wounds. "A fourteen-year-old boy killed that piece of shit, and he died crying like a girl."

Dempsey sucked back a hard breath, his chest expanding before he finally let it out with a short laugh. "Oh, you are going to fucking pay for that one."

Jolie barely let herself glance away from Dempsey, but when she did, it was to the sight of Red fighting back tears. He had color back in his face, but it was the same red color as his hair. And the blood that currently bloomed through his leather jacket and slowly dripped a trail down his clothes. There would be a puddle of blood there soon enough if Liam didn't get his claws out of Red's clothes and let him heal.

"Jolie, come on, you're not going to shoot me," Dempsey said, as if he really thought she wouldn't pull the trigger to defend herself.

It said a lot about what he thought of her.

"I will shoot you if you come near me," she threatened. The problem was she didn't know if she had it in her to kill him. Maybe Dempsey was right to not take her threat so seriously. That wasn't who she was. Jolie wasn't sure if it was the side of her that was an omega, or maybe something about her personality, but even now, her finger felt locked in front of the trigger.

As if she wouldn't be able to pull it even if she tried.

She really didn't want it to come to that. She just wanted

this idiot to turn around and walk away, leaving her and Liam alone.

"You need to go home, Dempsey."

He narrowed his eyes at her. His ice cold blue eyes staring into her soul almost, as if he was trying to freeze her from the inside out.

Despite all the times she'd pissed him off over the years, this had to be taking the freaking cake. This was the mother lode, and Jolie might have found the red line that he would rather she hadn't crossed. The ceiling for what she was allowed to get away with when it came down to it.

"Jolie, give me the gun, and tell that wild mutt to let go of Red."

Jolie wanted to laugh at that. "You heard him, he doesn't listen to me, and he's wild."

"You just told him not to kill Red," Dempsey said through gritted teeth.

"That's still up to him," Jolie replied, not taking her eyes away from Dempsey as she addressed Liam. "But please don't kill him anyway."

Liam made a gruff noise that she took to mean he would, reluctantly, do as she asked, but he didn't give it away to Carl, Dempsey, Patrick, or Dustin what the plan was.

Good. That was good.

Except Dempsey was still walking towards her, and Jolie backed into the water.

"Don't come near me," she warned.

"Jolie!" Liam yelled, throwing Red down hard onto the wet rock of the waterfall.

Patrick, Carl, and Dustin got between Liam and Jolie, leaving her alone to deal with Dempsey.

Shit! Shit, shit, shit! She'd thought for sure they had the upper hand, but Liam had only taken out Red. There were still the other three to deal with.

"I said stop moving!" Jolie yelled. Her heart pounded, and her tail was fighting to tuck itself between her legs.

"Uh huh, well I'm going to keep moving," he said, his eyes narrowed on her as he approached, slow and steadily. "You want to stop me then you're going to have to blow my brains out."

Jolie's stomach and lungs seized up within her. For a long, painful second, her heart stopped beating, and she couldn't breathe.

Jolie shook her head.

Dempsey shrugged. "What? Did you think I'd turn around and walk away? What kind of alpha do you think I am?"

"A crazy one?" she squeaked.

From the corner of her eye, she could see the way Liam prowled, trying to get through the other men, but they kept their guns locked on him. Liam roared at them, and for some miraculous reason, none of them shot.

Possibly because Dustin, Carl and Patrick had known Liam before the banishing. They didn't want to do this either.

Jolie definitely didn't want to do this.

"I don't want to be your mate, Dempsey."

He shook his head softly, his gaze never leaving the lock he had on her. "Not your choice, sweetness."

"Uh huh, well what if I told you that I'm Liam's mate? His natural one. I'll never want you the way I want him."

Dempsey's eyes brightened, and once again, that calm, cool exterior broke, and she saw the enraged animal within him.

He never could contain his rage for long before letting it out. It was made even scarier by the fact that he didn't say anything to her about that at all. He just kept walking forward.

"Jolie!" Liam roared.

He was changing into his wolf form. Out of the corner of her eye, she could see it, and it didn't matter if Patrick, Carl and Dustin had known him. They were going to kill him if they thought Liam was a danger to their lives.

Which he absolutely was. He'd said it himself that his animal form was on the wilder side. He didn't have the best control after years and years of living by himself. She needed to do something. She needed to act before someone else did.

Jolie pointed her weapon quickly to Dempsey's shoulder and she pulled the trigger.

A popping noise, and then he screamed and fell back, his hand coming up and clutching at his shoulder, bright red streaming through his clenched fingers as he fell down to his ass.

Liam lunged. More guns fired, but he didn't go after Carl, Dustin or Patrick, he ran through them, knocking both men off their feet and running towards Dempsey just as he started to shift into his own wolf shape.

And Jolie knew exactly what he was going to do.

She stepped in the way, her arms spread. "No!"

Liam's back paws came down hard. He kicked up rocks as he skidded to a complete halt before he could charge into her by accident. He lifted his muzzle, his lips still pulled back, revealing those long pointed teeth.

Patrick and Dustin no longer had their guns pointed at him. Carl did have his weapon still up, and the way his knees trembled said a lot for how lucky Liam was that he hadn't been shot after charging through the three men.

In fact, Carl looked very much like he was about to piss himself. The gun in his hand trembled, and any moment, he could squeeze the trigger a little too tightly. His aim probably wouldn't be right to get a kill shot, but it was still too much of a risk for Jolie to take.

She locked eyes with Liam, searched for any shred of his

humanity in there, and fuck. She had no idea if it was there or not.

"Can you recognize me right now, Liam? Can you hear me?"

Those pointed silver and black ears bent backwards. Liam's head bent, and his hackles raised up high as he growled at her again.

Jolie forced herself to breathe. She glanced back at Dempsey, who was pushing himself to his feet, growling and glaring at both her and Liam.

"You fucking bitch!" he snapped.

"Shut up, Dempsey, I'm keeping you alive." Jolie absolutely did not feel as confident as she sounded. She was definitely faking this. She had no idea what she was doing, and Liam could go on the warpath at any moment and decide to tear them all to pieces. He might end up killing her by accident, mate or no mate.

Much as she didn't want Liam to kill any of the men here, she was *really* concerned with what would happen to herself.

And what Liam would feel if he woke up out of this enraged state and found her in a bloody heap on the ground.

Somehow, that seemed like a worse fate, and she didn't want that for him. She didn't want him to come out of this fog he was lost in and find out he'd killed his own mate.

Jolie's tail was definitely fighting to get between her legs. She forced it not to as she called out to Carl, Patrick, and Dustin, never taking her gaze off of Liam.

"You guys take care of Red. The blood might set him off, make him want to target him. Get him out of here."

Again, she didn't feel any of this confidence that was in her voice. She should look into a career as an actress if she made it out of this relatively unscathed.

"Oh, fuck that, just shoot him!" Dempsey called.

Jolie slowly began walking sideways, getting out from

between Dempsey and Liam now that Liam didn't appear all that focused on Dempsey.

Also, it seemed smart to not keep him behind her. If he tried grabbing her, thinking to use her as a human shield, then regardless of whether or not Liam recognized her, the sudden movement might set him off.

From the corner of her eye, she didn't see Dustin, Carl, and Patrick getting a move on yet, but then they did slowly pull back.

Red breathed as if he only had a single working lung. At least Dustin was helping him to his feet. The three men not injured kept a protective circle around Red. Carl still had his weapon out, and all eyes were a bright shade of yellow.

They were alert, that was a good thing. Better to be alert and calm than enraged and trigger happy.

The problem was when Liam turned back to look at them, his large, black, wet nostrils flaring as he stared at his prey.

"Hey, hey, Liam, look at me, not them."

Shit, was he smelling Red's blood? That wasn't good. That was not good.

"Where the fuck do you think you're going?" Dempsey snapped. "Get back here now!"

"We can come back, we know how to get back," Dustin said, keeping his attention as much on Liam as he could.

"You'll come back here right now!" Fur sprouted on Dempsey's face. His eyes blazed to a bright red.

And now Jolie couldn't keep her tail from quivering between her legs. An angry alpha was never a good sign for an omega.

And Liam was rumbling. His fur actually rippled as he crouched down just a little lower, as though getting ready to spring.

"Liam, no, don't do it. Look at me, hey, come on, look at

me." She tried to keep her words as gentle as possible. She didn't want to scare him.

But when Liam looked at her, she realized that scare was probably the wrong word to think about when it came down to this.

Jolie swallowed hard.

Liam turned away from her, and he put his attention back onto Dempsey. Dempsey stared back at him, a hard expression, but Jolie caught the way his throat worked in a hard swallow, and the flicker in his eyes when he looked to Jolie.

"We could run. We could make it," he said.

Jolie frowned, and nearly fell back a step. "I'm not going with you." The fact that he could even still think that was an option was crazy as all hell.

"Now is not the time for you to get stubborn and stupid," Dempsey said through his teeth. "Look at him, he'll kill us both!"

Liam stalked towards Dempsey, and in that moment, he really did look like an animal, as if there was nothing remotely human inside his mind.

But Jolie wouldn't leave him.

"If you go, I can hold him back."

"*What?*" Dempsey's eyes were as wide as golf balls, though he didn't keep his attention on her for long before he started backing away from the enormous wolf that approached, as if it was getting ready to make an amazing kill.

"I think he can sense you're an alpha." Though Jolie didn't understand how that was happening with the way Dempsey kept backing up. Dempsey didn't turn his back to Liam, which was good. If he did, he was a dead man, but with every step forward Liam made, Dempsey took a step back, though now he was bending his knees, keeping his hands out. It was as if he was waiting for the moment when Liam sprung on him, so he could attack, or defend.

Probably getting ready to defend.

Jolie took the risk of slowly stepping up alongside Liam. He didn't seem to notice her. She made him notice when she pushed her fingers through his coarse grey fur.

That seemed to startle him, and Liam looked back at her, his eyes glowing, but his growl looked a touch less…growly, she supposed when he saw it was her.

He did know it was her. She'd been hoping for this, and now that she had it, she was glad for it. The relief was so much it was as if a real physical ache she'd been carrying around had finally stopped hurting so much.

Jolie breathed a sigh of relief, and she looked back up at Dempsey. "I'm sorry for tricking you, but I'm not going with you. I'm staying with him."

Dempsey shook his head. "No, he'll kill you if you stay with him."

"No, but he will kill *you*." She needed him to see that, to understand it for real this time. "If he attacks you, I won't be able to stop him, and Dustin and the others are getting Red out of here. You're by yourself."

"I'm an alpha."

"Yes, you are, and Liam is bigger and stronger than you are, and I can't control him."

She said it slowly, not because she thought Dempsey was stupid, but she definitely didn't want any of his alpha pride coming forward and getting him killed.

Seeing Red's blood had been enough. Her ears were ringing because of all the violence. She couldn't take anymore. She wanted to beg Dempsey to turn around and go back to Renzo, but she said nothing else.

If he did as she'd asked him to, he would do it now. He wouldn't wait any longer.

Dempsey growled. His eyes were such a bright shade of red that it had taken over his pupils. Jolie's heart stopped.

Holy shit. He was going to attack. He wasn't going to stop. He was going to come at her and Liam was going to kill him.

She waited, unable to breathe or move and already trying to think about how she could possibly change his mind and get him to stop.

Dempsey's shoulders bunched up and in that next moment, the tension released in a heaving sigh. He barely let himself look away from Liam. A man was never supposed to take his eyes off the enemy waiting to gut him from the front, never mind an alpha who wanted to bite off his face.

"I'll come back for you," Dempsey said, his fists clenched, looking to Jolie once more before glaring at the bear-sized wolf in front of him.

Jolie shook her head. "You wouldn't be saving me from anything, Dempsey. I want to be here."

Dempsey shook his head, but whether he believed it or not, Jolie wouldn't know, because he started to back away.

Liam made as if he wanted to follow, but Jolie fisted her hand into his fur. When the wolf felt the tug, he growled back at her, but at least he stopped following Dempsey.

Jolie shook her head. "You don't need his blood."

She prayed he listened.

Dempsey took another step back, and then another. Jolie didn't move and she wouldn't allow Liam to move either. Only when Dempsey was a fair enough distance away that he could get some real traction did he turn his back on his enemy, properly shifting into his wolf shape and running off.

Jolie still didn't move, and at least now Liam didn't seem to be fighting her on wanting to chase, though he did release what sounded to be a hard sigh.

"I know you want to kill him," Jolie soothed. "That's just too damned bad for you."

Liam growled back at her.

Jolie looked the wolf right in the eyes. She was the mate of a wild wolf. She'd set herself up for this, for the rest of her life. It was time for her to learn how to not back down when the wolf showed his teeth.

CHAPTER 10

It took about ten minutes before Liam stopped growling as if he was watching a squirrel get away from him.

And even then, Jolie was so paranoid he would want to chase after Dempsey, or Red, that she refused to let him go for another five minutes after that.

She figured, hoped, that they would be far enough away by then that a wolf eager to hunt wouldn't want to bother with them.

She released her grip on Liam's fur. Jolie hissed when she did so; the blood rushing back into her aching knuckles absolutely did not feel good.

At least Liam wasn't growling at her anymore. It was progress.

He definitely didn't look happy, though, so it wasn't as if she could feel overly safe and good about that.

"Liam? Please give me a sign you recognize me."

The wolf stepped forward. Jolie stepped back.

Those bright wolf eyes glanced down to her hand.

Jolie looked, and was shocked to see she still had

Dempsey's gun in her hand. Her knuckles were white as she gripped the handle, but her finger was not on the trigger. At least that was something good.

Liam made a soft noise deep in his throat. A groaning sound that got her attention, and made her understand what he was upset about.

She bent down, still keeping her movements slow and steady to keep herself from startling him. She let the gun settle on the ground before standing back up.

Liam sat down, his back straight and paws perfectly in front of him.

Jolie's heart pounded hard and fast, but in that moment, she couldn't help but look at him as if he was the most regal thing in the world.

He was beautiful. And alive.

"Are you…are you okay now?"

She didn't expect an answer. Part of her thought she would be handling Liam in his wolf shape for the next several hours before he came out of it. Not that it mattered so long as he wasn't attacking her or carrying her off by the scruff of her neck.

She just didn't think he would transform back into his human shape so suddenly, and be standing there in all his naked glory so soon.

Liam shook his body off, as if he was shaking out loose hairs. It was ridiculous to watch him do in his human shape, and Jolie laughed at the sight.

She needed to laugh after what she'd just been through.

When Liam looked at her, she couldn't make herself stop. "I'm sorry. Sorry, it was just funny watching you do that."

He rubbed his hand through his hair, which was long and loose, and a touch messy on the sexier side, around his shoulders. "Did you have to grab my fur like that?"

He asked it as if he wasn't finding the whole situation as

funny as she was. He sounded more put off about the whole thing.

Which was when she realized he'd spoken to her, as if he was in control, and as if he remembered what she'd been doing to him.

No faster way to get her serious and alert than to speak, apparently. "You…you were in control?"

"Barely," Liam growled, his eyes narrowing at her. "What the hell were you thinking getting in the middle of that? I could have killed you."

Jolie had to think about what he just said. "So, you got your control back when I got in the way?"

"You're lucky I did." He sounded furious. He looked it, too. His shoulders bunched up. Some of his veins popped and his fists were clenched hard enough that his arms trembled. "I nearly killed you. I might not have recognized your scent in time and I would have put my teeth around your throat and—"

Jolie rushed at him, shutting him up as she reached up, grabbed him by the ears and yanked his head down, crushing their mouths together.

The perfect way to shut him up.

Again, he seemed shocked to have her mouth on his, but like the last time, it had the desired effect. He was quiet, and then his body melted against hers, allowing her to mold their mouths together the way she wanted, the way she'd needed to ever since she'd found him.

That one little quick kiss she'd given to him before rushing out of their cave hadn't been nearly enough.

He was alive and well and he was himself. He could understand her. He was here with her and everything was going to be all right now because Dempsey was gone and it would be hours before he was able to come back.

This time, it would be with even more people than before

if he could get Renzo to sign off on it. That didn't matter now because the only thing in the world Jolie cared about was the taste of Liam's mouth.

She licked the crease of his lips, delighting in the way his mouth parted from the sudden shock of the touch, allowing her to teasingly lick at the inside, her tongue very briefly touching his.

She pulled back, too happy with herself for being brave enough to stand up to Dempsey, and with Liam for knowing who she was even when he clearly had been struggling for control.

"Your body is stiff."

Liam glared at her, the pointed ends of his fangs showing. "Of course it is when you kiss me like that."

Jolie barked a laugh, and had to quickly stifle it from the embarrassment of making a noise like that, but she couldn't help it. She could hardly contain it, even as she covered her mouth.

Jolie shook her head, getting control over herself. "I'm not talking about your...you know." She glanced down to his dick.

Yeah, it was stiff, and looking right up at her as if it had a mind of its own and wanted something from her.

Right, as much as she wanted to give in and put them both out of their misery, now wasn't the best time for that. They needed to get out of here.

"I was talking about the rest of your body," she said, taking Liam by his wrists and putting his hands onto her hips. "You're allowed to touch me when we're kissing like this."

"Are others allowed to touch you like this?"

"They'd have to be kissing me, and no one other than you is allowed to kiss me."

That got his attention nicely enough. Jolie noted the

sudden spark in his eyes, and the faint upward curl at the corner of his scarred mouth.

The grip of his hands tightened very briefly just then, and Jolie couldn't have been more proud in that moment.

"If Dempsey had touched you, tried to take you away, I wouldn't have been able to stop myself. You should know that."

Jolie nodded. lifting her arms and curling then neatly around his neck. They fit there so perfectly. "I know. We can deal with that. You're only a little wild. We can work with the rest."

"I have nothing to give you."

"Doesn't matter. I'll share what I've got and you can provide the muscle."

Liam growled at her again. "You're determined to be a pest, aren't you?"

She grinned up at him, her fingers twirling into his hair. "If by pest, you mean not put up with your self-pitying shit, then yes, absolutely." Liam rolled his eyes, that hard growl still on his mouth when Jolie grabbed him by the chin and made him look back at her. "Cut that out and kiss me. We don't have long before we have to get out of here. They'll be back."

Liam nodded. "And if they try to take you, I will kill them."

"Try not to."

"What will you do if I kill someone and can't stop myself?" he asked. "You wouldn't want to be with me then, would you?"

It was a valid enough question, and one Jolie realized she had to answer right now. "You're my mate," she said softly. "It took me long enough to come for you, and so long as you do your best to not kill anyone whenever possible, then if it happens, we'll deal with it then. I'll still be with you. I won't leave you alone again."

It seemed to be the *again* part that got to him the most. Jolie noted the hard movement in his Adam's apple as he swallowed, and the tension in his jaw when he nodded.

"I promise, that for you, I will do my best to not kill him, even though Dempsey deserves it."

Jolie wasn't sure if Dempsey did deserve it or not, but she wasn't going to argue with him about it right now. Not when they were so close to making peace on this.

Baby steps. Jolie was going to make baby steps, and this was enough progress that she could be happy.

"You're going to be a wild card, aren't you?"

Liam tilted his head to the side a little, as if he didn't fully understand her.

Jolie shook her head, smiling. "Never mind, I'll explain later, but right now we need to get you cleaned up and dressed if we're going to head into town."

Liam tensed. "Leave the pack?"

"Yes." She nodded. "And it'll be okay to leave because we have each other. There's a clan of bears not that far from here. We can ask to join then."

Liam's nostrils flared. He looked anything but happy about the thought of leaving the pack.

Even though he'd been kicked out of it, after how badly they had treated him after his father's death, it was still home.

"I don't want to leave it either, but Liam, you are my home now. I can be happy anywhere we go so long as you're alive and healthy and safe with me."

"It will be my job to make sure you are those things."

She smiled at that. "And I will be, just stay with me, please?" she begged.

He looked down at her. His hand came up, touching the softness of her wolf ear.

Jolie winced a little when he touched the hole Dempsey had punched into it.

Liam pulled his hand back, glancing at the blood on his fingers, and then at her. He nodded. "I will go with you. Anywhere you go, I will have to follow." He sighed. "The pack…you are half the reason I stayed. More than half. With you not there anymore, there's no point."

Jolie honestly felt as if she could cry. The sudden burn in her eyes hit her had. It was a struggle to hold back. "Really?"

Liam nodded, and there was something adorably innocent about how this powerful alpha could barely allow himself to look into her eyes in that moment. As if he was embarrassed to admit to this. "Yes."

Jolie couldn't contain herself. She bounced on her heels and had to kiss him again, so she did, and this time, Liam came down with a little less shock on his face, his mouth not quite as stiff as before.

He was getting better at this.

And the heat of the kiss, the sensation that this was the most right thing in the world, was still there.

Jolie was kissing her mate. She was kissing the man nature had chosen for her, and she would have never been given this feeling of excitement, and oddly enough, peace, had she ever been forced to kiss Dempsey.

"I'll take care of you, I promise," Jolie said between kisses. "Whatever you want, I'll get it for you, or help you get it."

If he was so worried about his job qualifications, she'd help him out with that. If he was concerned that he wouldn't be able to provide her with money, then she would be the one to provide it.

Liam seemed to have an opinion about this as he broke

off their kiss. "I will give you everything you want, too. I don't know how—"

"Doesn't matter how, just shut up and kiss me!" Jolie laughed, and then brought his mouth back down onto hers.

He melted against her, which was fine. It was preferred, actually, and Jolie let herself get swept away in the mouth of her mate.

Might as well enjoy this while they could. After this, they were going to have some real work to do.

THE END OF THIS STORY
NEXT: THE WILD WOLF'S WIFE VOLUME 2

CHAPTER 11

Jolie Farris was pretty much a walking stereotype when it came to what an omega was supposed to be. She didn't like blood, didn't often change into her wolf shape, and because of those first two facts, it meant she didn't like hunting either. The lack of practice made her pretty bad at it, as a matter of fact.

Something her stupid mate, Liam O'Connell, took absolutely no pity on her for. Which she hated him for. She loved him, but she hated him.

The enormous gray wolf stalking next to her was shockingly silent, despite his heavy paws.

Jolie was much smaller, smaller than even a natural wolf, and yet every step she took forward, putting her paws down onto the earth, seemed to crunch every dry leaf and twig possible.

The rabbit she hunted lifted its small brown head, ears tense, eyes alert.

Liam wouldn't let her hunt a moose or a deer. He'd growled that she was going to learn how to hunt if it was the last thing he did, but it seemed he was dead set against letting her near any animals that could potentially kill her if she spooked them.

They'd learned that the hard way the first time Liam brought them out.

Liam's ears flicked. He lowered himself down, as though getting ready to spring. His position reminded her more of a cat in that moment than a wolf, but he was better than she was at this by a long shot, so she didn't question it too much.

She just did as he did, rolling her shoulders, waiting for the fat rabbit over there to lower its guard. Why the hell did rabbits have to be so nervous all the time? It made it next to impossible to go after them when they were constantly a hair's-breadth from bolting.

Liam's tail smacked her on her butt, the signal she needed to get a move on.

She lunged. The shrubs she'd been hiding behind smacked her hard across her nose, scratching her and blinding her a little as she made her chase to catch her dinner.

That split second of no sight because she'd closed her eyes to keep the leaves and twigs out of them was more than enough for her dinner to scurry as if there was a small fire lit under it's fluffy ass. It wasn't beneath her claws when she landed, that was for damned sure.

Jolie lifted her snout, smelling the direction it bounced off into before she actually saw it, and she gave chase.

The damned thing bolted between trees, changing directions at lightning fast speed. Jolie circled around several large pines as it did. At one point, it even scurried over Liam's claws, apparently not noticing the larger wolf was just sitting there.

Jolie growled at Liam as she passed him by, and she could swear that even in his wolf shape, he was smiling at her.

He thought her failure was funny, huh? Well, she'd show him.

Jolie thought she didn't have any more bursts of speed to give, but she did. She pumped legs with a ferocity she didn't know she had. She was catching up! Its furry rump got ever closer and she opened her mouth and—

Pain and white exploded across the front of her head, just above and between her eyes. Right in the worst possible place. A wolf cry escaped her throat as she went down hard, her body sliding beneath the log she hadn't seen coming, the one the damned rabbit had raced beneath to get away from her.

If its little trick had been on purpose, then she should congratulate it for its cleverness. The cunning scheme worked.

She shifted, changing back into her human shape, almost against her will, as if the wolf side of her brain was desperate to hide away from the pain she'd just inflicted on the both of them.

"Oh God," she moaned, bringing her hands up to her forehead. She felt something warm and wet there.

Don't be blood. Don't be blood. Don't be blood.

She brought her hands back down, and of course it was blood. Honestly, what did she think it was going to be?

"Jolie?"

Liam's voice was a blessing and a total curse because the sound of it was enough to make her brain throb harder than before.

She closed her eyes as he ducked beneath the heavy log, his hands reaching out for her. He didn't move her, but he touched her wrists, his hands sliding up her arms and to her shoulders. He was like that. He seemed to check on her with his hands instead of his eyes whenever he thought something was wrong.

"Are you all right?"

"Head hurts," she moaned, and it was an honest to God fight to keep her eyes from burning too much. She wanted to cry from the pain, but if she started shedding tears in front of Liam, he might change his mind about wanting her to hunt.

She hadn't wanted to learn how to hunt necessarily, but if this was going to stop, then at the very least she wanted it to be on her own damned terms. Not because Liam suddenly thought she couldn't handle it.

"You're bleeding. I need to get you out of here."

"Where the hell did that stupid tree come from?" she grumbled, managing to get her eyes open and stare at the offending thing above her.

"I imagine it's been here for a while now," Liam said.

When her vision stopped trembling, Jolie could see the moss growing on it, the way the termites had eaten away at much of the bottom, and there were a few spiders frantically scrambling back to their crevices and webs, away from the commotion.

It was big enough that it was as if there was a roof two feet above her head. She wouldn't have run into it if the earth hadn't dipped the way it did.

She and Liam were actually fairly hidden here.

"I'm going to move you," he said, his hands coming beneath her back and legs. "Try not to tense up."

"Ugh." Easier said than done. It was as if the second his hands touched her, the flaring pain in her head woke up a monster even worse.

Despite the limited space Liam had to work with, he managed to pull her out from beneath the fallen log fairly quickly, but then Jolie covered her eyes with her hand because the limited light, even through the canopy above her head, was doing its best to stab her right in the retinas.

"I'll take you back to the motel. Don't worry."

"You can't run around like this."

She was dressed, but Liam didn't like to wear clothes when he knew he was going to make a shift. To him, it didn't seem to matter if the clothes changed with his body, he complained that it didn't *feel* right.

Which meant that if anyone happened to see them, they wouldn't see an oversized wolf with a smaller wolf running next to it, they would see a naked man carting off a bleeding woman in the woods. It might invoke some sort of horror story images in anyone who happened to come across that.

But as Liam started to run with her in his arms, it was the last thing she was suddenly concerned with as every step he made brought the hammer down harder on her skull.

"Oh God, stop running so fast."

"I'm barely jogging," he said, but he did slow down. She supposed he was walking now, but even then, the pain in her front temple was the absolute worst. She grit her teeth against it, but it didn't seem to be enough to hold back the pain.

Suddenly, she didn't care who saw them like this, so long as it wasn't Dempsey, Renzo, or anyone else from the pack who wanted to take her back, then she could handle it. She'd make up some lie about what they'd been doing out here, just so long as she got some bandages and ibuprofen.

Jolie spent most of the journey back gritting her teeth and clutching her head, both to hold back the pain and to keep too much more blood from spilling, so she didn't notice when they made it back to the motel they were staying at along the highway.

"I'm sorry I couldn't do it," she said softly as Liam walked across the parking lot to their door.

"Don't worry about it. I'll get you something to eat later on tonight. Do you have the key?"

Jolie fished through her pockets, had a near panic attack

when she couldn't find the key right away, and sighed when her fingers finally touched the metal. She pulled it out and handed it to him. "Make sure you get dressed," she said, smiling when she opened the door for them.

He answered her with a gruff snorting noise. She was pretty sure that was a no. He wouldn't be getting dressed for her just then.

Liam set her on the bed with gentle care, but he could have dropped her on it for all it mattered with the way her brain matter screamed out, as if it was about to burst inside her skull. When he pulled his hands away from her, the room spun, as if she was lying in a small boat in a body of water.

Liam went into the bathroom, still not dressed. When he came out with a small first aid kit, she was impressed the motel would even have one of those.

He set it onto the bed. The supplies he pulled out were ho-hum exciting, mostly small bandages and the tiniest bottle of peroxide she'd ever seen in her life. He'd brought a clean rag from the bathroom with him, wet it with the peroxide, and then began dabbing at her temple.

"Is it bad?" she asked.

"Not sure. You're not spurting blood, so that's good news."

She smiled up at him. "Renzo always said I have a thick skull."

"He did?"

"Not in those words, but I'll say that he did because it fits nicely into the story." Jolie hissed as his next gentle dab got her harder than needed.

"Sorry," Liam said, his voice gentle. "You might have a concussion. I don't know how to treat that."

"Are my ears out?"

"Yes. Your tail, too."

Jolie cursed. There was no way she was going to a hospital like that.

"Can you put them away?"

She tried. "Are they gone?"

"No, and your tail is thumping the bed now."

He sounded somewhat amused to say that. Jolie wasn't amused. She was frustrated. She wanted to be able to do more than just lie here, injured and helpless. Helpless meant their chances of staying on the run if Renzo came after them took a nose dive. Helpless meant that Liam had to do more work than he already needed to do.

Helpless meant he was in even more danger than he already was. She knew he would leap over her body to protect her if she couldn't protect herself.

That was mostly already true. She was an omega, and fairly weak even by omega standards, but she did know how to run.

Running was how she'd found Liam again.

"I'll hunt you something to eat," he said.

"Or I could order Chinese food," Jolie suggested.

Liam shook his head. "No, save your funds for your shelter and medicine. Those things are more important."

Jolie wanted to argue, but she knew he was right. She just hated that he was.

"Never should have told you how much cash I have."

He smiled at her, something that looked almost mischievous. "Too late for that now. You're providing all of this," he said, looking around the motel room they were in as if it was a magical palace. "I will provide your protein so you can eat."

Jolie tried to smile for him, but she got the feeling the *smile* looked more like a grimace. "I promise I didn't do that on purpose," she said. It seemed important that he know this. "I don't like hunting, but I wouldn't give myself a concussion to get out of it."

She was also smart enough to know that he'd wanted her to learn just in case he couldn't do it for her. In case she had to keep running without him. She couldn't think of any situation in which that would have been necessary, any situation in which she would leave him behind, but she'd appreciated the thought he'd put into her care.

Getting her head thwacked while chasing after Bugs Bunny had definitely not been part of the plan.

"Don't worry about it, just get better."

Liam shocked her when he leaned down, pressing his mouth to her lips. The kiss itself didn't shock her. The gentle sweetness of it did.

Usually, whenever he kissed her, there was a fire in his mouth, a passion and energy put into it, as if he couldn't bring himself to keep his mouth parted from hers for any longer.

Gentle kisses were…uncommon. That much was enough.

"I'll go get you something," he said, then sighed. "I'll have to get dressed for it."

She lifted her brows. "You're going to order the food?"

"No, but I'll need to keep the door locked when I leave. I'll have to keep the key in my pocket."

It was funny the way he sounded miserable about that, as if that was the last thing in the world he wanted to do.

It hurt like hell, but Jolie couldn't help but laugh at him.

Except for when the door banged open, and an enormous red wolf burst into the room.

CHAPTER 12

The sound of the door smashing in was enough to make Jolie jump, but the pain in her skull was enough that even the danger couldn't make her get out of bed, especially when she realized who the red wolf could be.

"Goddamn it, Red!" she yelled, then hated herself for making the pain in her skull throb that much harder. She fell back onto the bed, her hands clutching her temples, as if that was going to keep the pain at bay.

It totally didn't, and then there was nothing but growling and snapping as something else crashed in the motel.

Fuck, was that the TV? She didn't dare open her eyes, and she sure as hell didn't want to see how much furniture was getting destroyed as Liam and Red rolled around the room. Somehow, they managed to form an arc around her bed, bumping into it and knocking her around only occasionally, but she ignored it, clutching at her head, fairly sure she was starting to bleed all over again from the intense pulsing happening in her brain.

Jolie rolled onto her side, clenching her teeth while squeezing her eyes shut tighter. If she willed them both to go away enough, would they do it? Would someone answer her wish and make both wolves vanish out of here so she could start recovering in peace?

Something else crashed, sounded like a lamp, and the sharp whine Red let out was nearly enough to make her open her eyes. She didn't.

"Liam, don't hurt him too much," Jolie groaned.

Red's voice was high-pitched and offended. "How do you know it's me he's got?"

She didn't bother to look back at them. "Obviously it's not him."

Liam must have still been in his wolf form, at least if the sound of his chuckle was anything to go by. He definitely sounded as if he was a big animal with some prey between his teeth when he let out that noise.

"Okay! Okay! I'm sorry! *Liam!*"

Jolie couldn't stand to hear Red scream like that. She groaned, forcing herself up and to her feet. Every step she took was another nail hammered into the side of her skull, but she made it to the door and slammed it shut, a noise that vibrated through the inside of her cranium like a golf ball bouncing around an enclosed space.

Liam turned back into his human shape. She only knew this because she heard his voice as she stumbled blindly back to bed.

"Jolie! You shouldn't be walking around."

"I know," she moaned, gently crawling back onto the mattress and easing herself down. "Please stop yelling."

"I'm not yelling."

It super sounded like he was yelling, unless that was just in her head. Holy shit. Was it in her head? She pulled the pillow over her skull, and even with their voices slightly muffled, she could still make out everything they said. Apparently she was getting sensitive to sound as well as light. The darkness within her new pillow cave seemed to help.

"What happened to her?"

"I took her hunting. It didn't end well," Liam growled.

Jolie's heart swelled just a little when he didn't explain to Red that she'd slammed her head into a tree.

"Jesus, was it Dempsey?"

"No, there was...an accident."

Jolie would kill him later. Why the hell did she have to love him so damned much when he was clearly an uncivilized asshat?

"Dempsey isn't with you?"

"No," Red said, muttering. "He was. We all basically know you're here. You've been here for days."

"Hmm," Liam said.

Jolie cringed beneath her pillow.

Maybe he wasn't such an asshat after all, considering she was the one who didn't want to move on just yet.

It had been Jolie's plan to stay on the highway a little longer. She'd even washed some dishes at the gas station diner for a little extra cash. Liam hadn't wanted her to do that, and had even claimed she didn't need to. He'd insisted that if they stayed in their wolf shapes, they could get to their destination within a couple of days.

Jolie hadn't been convinced she could make a trip like that in just her wolf shape, hunting exclusively for food, and sleeping outdoors.

She supposed she'd proved her point while chasing down what was meant to be her lunch, but she really wished it hadn't come down to that.

"So you broke in here to fight me for her, was that it?" Liam asked, a small possessive growl to his voice.

Jolie smiled beneath her pillow. She had never liked it when Dempsey had tried getting possessive over her. It had annoyed her more than anything, actually. When Liam got into the whole *my woman* sort of mood, it was easy to admit to herself that she liked it.

A lot.

"*No!* I mean…yeah. But I don't want to!"

"Didn't learn your lesson from the last time? Your shoulder doesn't look entirely healed yet."

Even though she was an omega, and even though she had that pillow over her head, Jolie could almost smell the fear coming from Red. Fear tended to smell like sweat, coupled with tiny droplets of pee. Red was definitely starting to smell like a little of both.

Jolie groaned over the whole thing. "Liam, leave him alone. He's our friend."

She had to be careful, even the sound of her own voice seemed to be dead set on sending painful vibrations all up and down the back of her skull

Liam growled a low and dangerous noise that had the small hairs on her arms stand up. "He works for Dempsey and wants to bring you back so you can mate with him."

"I *don't* want that," Red insisted. "But what the hell am I supposed to do? Renzo is my alpha."

"And she is my mate," Liam hissed.

Jolie pulled the pillow off her head just enough so she could see what her knight in shining armor was doing.

Mostly it involved showing his teeth off to poor Red while he pointed a clawed finger at the bed where Jolie was trying to rest and recover.

"*My* mate," Liam hissed again. "Not Dempsey's. I'll kill him before I let him touch her."

She smiled again. Yeah, Liam, unlike Dempsey, did the possessive thing right.

"What should we do with him?" Jolie asked, tenderly setting her head onto the pillow this time. She still hissed a little as the throbbing became almost too much to bear.

"Do with me?" Red asked, his voice trembling just a little.

Jolie was getting a bit more used to the light in the room. It was easy to see how terrified he was to take his eyes off Liam.

She snuggled onto the tough pillow, her tail curling around her. "Well, like you said, Renzo is your alpha. You're loyal to him unless you pledge your allegiance to another alpha. We can't exactly let you go if you're going to run back to Renzo."

Red's entire body tensed. "B-but I already told you he knows you're here!"

Liam made that growling noise as he spoke again. "And you're going to tell us everything you know about what he's been up to. Is he just watching us or is he plotting something? Does he want revenge? Does he still want Jolie for Dempsey?"

Jolie frowned at something just then. "And why did you break in to our room? That makes no sense."

If Renzo knew they were here and just wanted her and Liam watched for now, then the last thing Red should have done was bust down the door like he'd done. He might as well have picked up a megaphone and announced to the entire world what Renzo and Dempsey were doing.

And Red wasn't that stupid.

"Red," Jolie said again, forcing herself to sit up so she could really look at him. "Why did you come here? Does Renzo know?"

"Yes," Red said, sounding almost as if he was…pouting.

No. Effing. Way.

She and Liam looked at each other. Ever since she'd found him, and they both decided to act on their mating, something had clicked between them where they could just look at each other and know there was an agreement between them.

Liam turned his attention back to Red, though it didn't appear as if he was going to loosen his grip on the man's throat any time soon.

"All right, so you wanted my attention, you got it. What do you want?"

Red's eyes flew wide, and then he glared at Liam. "I never said I wanted your attention!"

Jolie brought her fingers up to massage her temple, grimaced, and pulled her hand back down. Great, she was bleeding again. "So, what? You just broke down the door without thinking through what you were going to do after that? That makes no sense."

"Are you bleeding again?" Liam asked.

"No."

It was too late. Jolie heard the outraged shout as Liam threw Red down and rushed to her side. His callused fingers somehow managed to be gentler than she could ever be as he pushed her hair out of her face to have a look at the wound.

"I'm fine," Jolie insisted.

"I know," Liam said, but that didn't stop him from putting the damp cloth back to her wound and dabbing the blood.

"Jesus," Red said, his brows furrowing as he looked down at her. "You hit your head bad, huh?"

She smiled. Might as well get over the embarrassment of it. "I'm a terrible hunter. I'll have to leave that to Liam if we're ever going to make a life together."

Red was silent at those words. Liam's hand touched her shoulder. It was warm and comforting, and she couldn't help but reach up and put her fingers on top of his.

It didn't even matter that there was someone watching their tender moment. The only thing Jolie cared about was that Liam was here.

And that she might have one of her friends back.

"Red, if you really want to help us, swear allegiance to Liam."

She felt the tension in Liam's touch when those words left her mouth. She saw the strain in Red's body after she spoke.

"I don't have a pack that could offer him protection if we were to ever go to war with anyone," Liam said, his voice getting all growly. "I can barely protect you."

Which was why he wanted her to know how to hunt for herself. She knew that now.

"What if we didn't have to search out the bear clan?" Jolie asked. "What if you just took back the pack? They might follow you. You're the son of the original alpha."

And a pretty badass alpha himself.

Which made her look at Red. "I think when you injured Red, you switched something inside him."

"No he didn't," Red insisted, crossing his arms and wincing only a little, as though the wound in his shoulder was still tender as he pulled it.

She smiled, because she knew he was lying. Jolie was a terrible shifter in general, but she was pretty good at reading people. It was a skill she'd had to work on with the way she was brought up in the pack, moving from couch to couch, keeping her distance from Dempsey…

"I think Red wants to be your beta," Jolie said. "You impressed him when you overpowered him outside the waterfall."

"No he didn't."

"So he tried to impress you by rushing in here and giving you a good fight."

"That it *not* how it was going down."

But Jolie could definitely tell she'd put him into a corner. Liam stared at the man, a single brow raised up high, and Red was refusing to look at any of them.

His face was turning a shade darker than his hair. It was enough to hide the freckles on his nose. It could have been anger, or embarrassment, but Jolie definitely knew he wasn't telling the truth.

"I know we're asking you to do a dangerous thing," Jolie said. "And maybe you weren't ready for this right now, but if you wanted to be on our team, and help keep Renzo off our backs until Liam is ready to challenge him, we would really appreciate it."

"I thought we were going to that bear clan?" Liam asked.

Jolie glanced up at him, smiling softly. She reached for his hand again, threading their fingers together. "Yeah, but I know that's not really what you want to do."

It wasn't. He hated the fact that he'd been exiled from his pack and he'd hated that he didn't have the ability to fight back.

He was outnumbered, packless, and he had no claim to even demand a fight for the role of alpha.

Rogues who tried to fight for the right to a pack on their own were always turned away. No matter how strong the challenger was, no one would come up against an entire pack if the standing alpha did not want to fight.

Which they never did.

Unless Liam had a pack of his own. Even a small one and he would be considered a legitimate challenger, and Renzo would have to take him seriously.

Liam seemed to be considering her words. His intense gaze flicked between Jolie, Red, and back again. His eyes changed color. A bright golden yellow. He was alert. Thinking.

Red looked guilty, and sorry as he backed up a step.

"I'm getting out of here," he said. "I shouldn't have come. They'll be pissed off when they smell me and know where I've been."

Liam didn't get up to follow Red to the door, and Red continued to back away slowly, never turning his back, as if he expected Liam to attack if he did.

He reached for the broken door, which couldn't even close properly. He yanked it open, nearly tearing it off its hinges just before he threw himself outside.

Jolie caught the brief sight of his clothes vanishing and fur appearing as he shifted and made his escape.

It didn't matter. She already had a much better plan.

CHAPTER 13

Jolie's head still spun, but she couldn't stop herself from playing out her brilliant plan over and over. Even after Liam dragged her out of her motel room so he could go and get his revenge on the bunny that had given her this injury in the first place, which was a miserable experience, she couldn't stop herself from getting excited.

"I wish you would lie down," Liam said, watching as she bounced around the motel room.

"Right, well, should have thought of that before you took me out hunting with you," she said, though she wasn't in a bad mood about it. She was still thinking over her plans; her wolf ears and tail had popped out and they didn't seem to want to go back in.

"If we can get just a couple more of the guys to go along with this—"

"They're not going to, Red was just testing the waters and he didn't like what he saw," Liam said, then crossed his arms and growled. "And I took you out of the room because we're being watched. I wasn't about to leave you alone."

Jolie scratched at the bandage wrapped around her temple. Liam had managed to find her one in the main office, and it was lucky no one had noticed the broken door yet. She didn't want to get kicked out of here just yet, especially when she was still working through her new plans, though at this point it was obvious their hours here were numbered.

"Stop picking at it."

She lowered her hand, pouting at him. "It itches, and this can definitely work. No one really respects Renzo. I mean, they respect his strength enough to follow him, but people still remember what he did. You can totally take him."

"Respect for his strength is most everything that's needed to lead a pack. Even if I decided to challenge him, and beat him, he still has something I don't."

Jolie felt her inner hackles rising up. "Oh yeah? And what's that?"

Liam stared her dead in the eyes. "Intelligence."

Jolie's eyes popped wide. She opened her mouth. Nothing came out, so she closed it again. There was nothing she could say to that. Not really. She tried anyway. "You're not stupid, Liam."

"No." He shook his head. "But I also don't have much of an education either. I could never manage the pack's finances, collect the funds from the people living in the pack and redistribute it fairly. I don't know how to fix a roof or repair plumbing, and I wouldn't know the right sentences to give out should anyone break pack law. I've been living out in the wild for too many years. Sometimes I can barely control my inner wolf. Red might *want* to have me as an alpha, but he knows these things just as much as I do. That's why he ran in the end."

Jolie shook her head, and her heart hurt for him. It throbbed and ached in a way she only seemed to feel whenever it came down to what Liam was feeling.

"You're not nothing, Liam," she said. Then she clenched her fists, letting herself get angry. "And who cares if you don't know how to do those other things? You can learn. I can help you. I can keep the pack's books and you can trust me if I ever tell you that you're being too harsh in your sentencing."

"You're still assuming I would challenge Renzo for the pack." Liam's eyes flashed to red. He looked away from her, as if he didn't want her to think it was her he was angry with. "The pack could have backed me then, when I killed Dempsey's idiot father after that prick murdered my mother. They let Renzo banish me instead of taking a stand then." Liam's jaw clenched, and it wasn't lost on Jolie how his claws started to come out at the memory he described. "Far as I'm concerned? They can have him."

It seemed so wrong to hear that coming from his mouth. Not just the words, but the way he said them. "But they're still your pack. You're an alpha; you can't really want to run away from them."

Liam met her eyes again, the red staying in place. "Don't mistake the fact that I stuck around the pack to mean I was loyal to *them*. I stayed close to the pack for one reason and one reason only. For *you*."

Jolie's heart did that painful palpitating thing again. She had to rub her chest, just over her heart, to make the aching stop.

Liam caught the action. Both brows lifted above his green eyes. "It hurts you that I don't want anything to do with the pack? You do remember they turned their backs on me."

"So did I," Jolie said, though she hated having to remind him of that fact.

Mostly because of how much she hated the truth in it.

Liam turned away from her. His eyes briefly flashed to red again.

When she'd first found him, he'd been furious with her. He hadn't wanted to admit they were mated at all, even though Jolie knew he'd been able to feel that pull as much as she had.

He'd stayed for her, but over the years he'd resented her a little. He'd never said it to her, but Jolie knew it was the case. It was pretty hard to hide something like that when he'd grabbed her by the throat in the cave behind the waterfall.

"You forgave me. Why can't you forgive them?" Jolie stepped up to him. She reached up, putting her hands on his bare shoulders. He was only in a pair of jeans, his feet bare, and he seemed absolutely determined to not look her in the eyes. And something unsettling occurred to her just then. "Liam, I am forgiven, right? I mean, are you still mad at me?"

They hadn't exactly worked out the details on what had been done, what she had done, considering Dempsey had attacked Liam's small home, forcing them on the run.

"I do," he said shortly, nodding.

"Then why won't you look at me?"

He did, finally. His green eyes looked very much as though they were struggling to stay their natural color.

Jolie's stomach did a strange, painful twist. She pulled her hands back.

Liam sighed, and he reached out to take her wrists before she could do something completely foolish, like step away from him entirely. "I've forgiven you. I just don't like what happened."

"Okay," Jolie said, her heart hammering so hot and heavy she felt the pulsing in her ears. "But you need to talk to me about these things. I know you were mad at me—"

"Not anymore," Liam said quickly.

"But that's not the point."

"Then what is the point?" Liam asked, and this time he sounded somewhat impatient. There was a growl in his voice, red in his eyes, and his lip curled as he released her wrists and turned away from her. "I don't understand you."

Jolie tensed. "Me?" She stared at Liam's back, wondering if it was even possible to hear something so utterly backwards. "You're the one that's hard to understand. Trust me." She tried to laugh about it, to joke it off, but the muscle in Liam's back tensed, as if he didn't enjoy the reminder of how new they both were to all of this.

They'd been best friends as kids. Liam's parents had taken Jolie in, before Renzo killed his father and took over the pack. Jolie could still remember the cracks in his mother's fierce strength slowly but surely starting to show as the shifter she was paired up with after the death of her husband hurt her.

Again and again.

Dempsey hadn't cared what his father did, and in truth, Jolie hadn't noticed his eyes on her even back then. She'd been too focused on trying to keep Liam from doing something dangerous.

When Liam killed his step father, Jolie was secretly glad he was dead. She only wished Liam had done it before the man had killed Liam's mother.

Then Liam was banished, and she had been on her own.

She looked hard at the back of Liam's head. She'd recently convinced him to let her cut his hair. The trust needed for an alpha to allow anyone to get near his face, head, and throat with a blade was monumental. She'd thought they'd made progress when he'd finally agreed to let her do it.

But really, how well did they honestly know each other? Seven years was a long time to be separated from each other, a long time for a boy to grow into a man in the wild...

How many people had Liam made contact with in the time he'd been away? A couple? Or none at all?

And something even more horrifying than all that struck her.

What if this wasn't just a shield he was putting up to protect himself with her? What if this was who he really was? Someone who kept people at an arm's length, even his mate, because he just didn't know how to interact with the people around him?

Jolie's throat closed. She inhaled a deep breath once, and then twice, working through the pain that struck her hard.

He wouldn't appreciate being pitied, so she would keep it to herself. But as much as she tried to bury the feeling, it was still there, and it made her look at him differently.

Jolie stepped forward. She hesitated only briefly, part of her wondering how welcome an act like this would be as she curled her arms around his waist from behind.

Liam's body tensed. "What are you doing?"

"I love you," Jolie said softly, squeezing him as tightly as she could. "I know things are different, I'm sorry I destroyed the life you built for yourself, but I'm still glad you're here, and if you don't want to talk about what happened, or what you're feeling, then I won't push you into doing that. I won't push you into trying to fight for the pack either. If you really want to be without them, then I'm with you."

"You say that now," Liam grumbled.

"And I mean it." She looked up at the back of his head, trying desperately to make him feel her sincerity. "You are my home now. I knew I probably wouldn't be going back when I ran away. I was fine with that then, and I'm fine with it now."

"You could always change your mind."

Jolie sputtered. "And go back to where Renzo wants to hand me over as some kind of prize to Dempsey?" Now she was growling. "No thanks."

Liam laughed. He...actually laughed. He turned in her

arms and looked down at her, his green eyes dancing in a way she hadn't seen since they were kids.

She kept glaring up at him. "I mean it. I'm not going back there if you're not going. I guess I just...brought it up because the idea of you being the rightful alpha and taking your place seemed kind of...poetic. Like that was the way things were supposed to be."

Especially when Red showed up and put those ideas into her head.

Maybe she was more connected to that pack than she'd thought she was. Despite the shortcomings, some of which were pretty big, it was still her home. It felt weird to leave it behind.

"Do you really think I'll change my mind on you?" Jolie noted the tension in his shoulders. It was answer enough.

She reached up and smacked him on the back of the head.

"Hey!" Liam yanked himself out of her arms, his expression more shocked and offended than anything else. "Did you just *hit* me?"

"Yeah, that's what you get for thinking I'd ever want to go back to that pack without you." Jolie stuck her hands on her hips. "Seriously, what do you think I am?"

"An abusive woman?"

Jolie blinked. "Uh, did I seriously hurt you?"

He was the one who did all the hunting. He stayed up late protecting her, making sure he didn't catch any familiar scents getting close to their room. Maybe he'd hurt himself at some point and just wasn't telling her? Maybe he...

The quirk at the corner of his lips snapped her out of it quickly, and then she wanted to strangle him. She actually tried to do just that, but Liam was smart, backing away from her whenever her hands got anywhere near his throat.

"I'm going to murder you! Are you serious?"

He wasn't laughing at her, not exactly, but he did smile

wider than she'd seen him smile in such a long time. It was almost strange to look at, and even though she still wanted to wrap her fingers around his neck and squeeze, soon, she couldn't stop laughing as she chased him around the motel room.

Her headache came back and throbbed like crazy as she hunted her mate, but it was too funny watching him hop over the bed, putting it between their bodies where she wouldn't be able to get at him.

And he was crazy. He was so damned crazy, and she was still in love with him.

Which was why she tried to jump over the bed to get him, only to have her klutziness rear its clumsy head as her feet got caught in the sheets and—how was that even possible?—she fell on her face.

She scrambled to her hands and knees. Liam wasn't about to let her have that advantage. He quickly climbed on top of her, turning her to her back and pinning her down, pressing her hands down hard on either side of her head.

"You're going to hurt yourself," Liam said, though it sounded as if he was still laughing at her.

Jolie blew the hair out of her face, which didn't help the headache that started to sink in, but all the same, she was still having fun.

"Yeah, I bet you're so worried about how much my head hurts when you're pinning me down."

"A little," Liam admitted. "Isn't having a headache the usual excuse?"

"For what?" Jolie asked, then felt stupid as she realized exactly what he was talking about.

They stared at each other, and in that moment, Jolie felt the warmth of his body pulsing much hotter than it should have, much more intensely than just three seconds ago when they were still playing around.

And through the denim of his jeans, she felt that heat collecting in one place in particular, and the firm length of his cock beneath the material pressed against her leg from the positions they held wasn't lost on her either.

Jolie swallowed, and an excitement shuddered through her as Liam's eyes changed to a bright shade of golden yellow.

Alert. Aroused.

"Your eyes are gold," Liam said.

Jolie nodded. "Yours too."

God, it felt as if she could hardly take a breath. Their motel room had turned into a sauna, and the only thing that could combat against the heat was his mouth.

Her gaze fell to his lips. He took the hint.

Liam kissed her. His lips were pillow soft on her mouth, and yet the stubble around his lips scratched her pleasantly. He never did like to shave all that often; that was fine. Jolie found that every time he kissed her, she grew to love the stubble more and more.

And unlike her previous hypothesis, being kissed by Liam while he held her down on the bed absolutely did not make the heat simmer down. It flared to life, like a living dragon inside her body, breathing fire all along the underside of her skin. A fire that travelled through her blood and bones, down her arms and legs. Liam moaned softly, his tongue slipping out and teasing her along the crease of her lips.

She opened for him, mewling softly, pushing her breasts forward, wanting his hands on them instead of her wrists, though she did like being held down.

The fire in her body pooled in her belly when his tongue slipped inside her mouth, swirling against hers, coaxing her to participate. She did to the best of her ability, but it didn't seem like nearly enough. It felt more as if she was desperately trying to keep up with him, something she could barely seem to do as she helplessly sucked on his tongue, feeling the throb of his cock through his jeans against her leg.

Jolie's sex swelled and flooded with heat. She wanted it inside her. The idea of sex had always bothered her, mostly because she'd suspected over the years that Dempsey would be the one to take her first time, but this was different.

This was Liam. Her best friend and her mate. She wanted him inside her and wanted it like *yesterday*.

Jolie pushed against his hands. She needed to move her arms. She wanted to wrap them around the back of his neck and hold on tight. She wanted to *touch* him.

Liam once again got the hint. He released her wrists, keeping himself propped up on his elbows as she dug her fingers into his hair. In that moment, she wished she hadn't cut his hair because, if she hadn't, there would be so much more of it to grab onto, and that would have been wonderful.

The hard groan Liam released when she fisted his hair vibrated into her mouth, making her body buzz, come alive.

And the pool of heat that surrounded her showed absolutely no signs of slowing down, of vanishing. It just got worse with every second, with every stroke of Liam's tongue.

Liam's large, powerful hand finally cupped her breast through her shirt, and she felt as if the heat of his palm was on her bare skin.

Maybe she shouldn't describe the sensation, the pleasure and heat, as getting worse. As it stood right now, this felt like it was just getting better and better.

And a wild, instinctual side of herself that Jolie never knew she had came to life. She lifted the leg that was still free, curling it around Liam's waist, just above the swell of his ass. She almost wished she could see what they looked like, especially as Liam groaned when she adjusted her other thigh, gently, trying to stroke the firm bulge she felt between Liam's legs with her knee.

He tensed at first, and then there was another powerful rumble through his body as he moaned against her mouth.

She soaked it in, pleased with herself that she could make him feel so good, the pleasure still building within her as she thrust against him, searching for a friction of her own.

And it was *perfect*. It was just the two of them, the way it was supposed to be.

Jolie managed to yank her hands out of Liam's hair. Her fingers scrambled down to the waist of his jeans.

She could have kicked herself for pressuring him into wearing pants while indoors. He would have already been naked if he'd just ignored her…

She reached down too far, her hand cupping over the bulge in his pants, and he jumped back suddenly.

Jolie blinked, surprised. "I'm sorry."

Though she would have thought touching him there would have been fine, especially right now.

All traces of the lust she'd seen in his eyes were gone. They were no longer golden. They were a bright shade of angry red.

"They're coming. Get your things."

CHAPTER 14

Jolie scrambled off the bed. She didn't have much to grab, just the bag of small things she'd managed to collect over the short period of time they'd been on the road. Food, some medical supplies they'd picked up after she'd hit her head, some toiletries, and an extra change of jeans and underwear—for her since Liam didn't wear too many clothes.

All things they could live without if they absolutely had to leave them behind, but she wanted to keep them with her. The pepper spray would also be helpful, considering how bad she was at defending herself.

Liam didn't grab his shoes, so Jolie did, stuffing them into the bag and slinging it over her shoulder just as Liam yanked the door open, his eyes still blazing red, his claws out and his teeth looking more like they belonged to a saber-toothed tiger than a wolf.

"You remember the plan?" he asked, not looking back at her.

"Yeah," she said, her heart still pounding. "I'll meet you down the road at the first gas station."

The map in her bag would lead her there. Liam had already memorized the locations of the next five gas stations. They'd planned this out for the possibility of being separated, but Jolie still thought she was going to have a heart attack.

"Good, now run. I'll meet you down the road."

"Wait!"

Liam stopped himself before he could rush out the door and into a fight.

He looked back at her just as Jolie grabbed onto his shoulders, pushing herself to her toes and kissing him on the mouth.

God, she wished they hadn't been interrupted. "Stay safe."

Liam blinked, his eyes still red, but there was something wide-eyed and innocent about his expression. The thin tint of red that colored his cheeks as he cleared his throat and turned from her let Jolie know all she needed to know. "You, too," he said, and then flew out of her arms and towards...whoever it was that was out there.

If anyone had seen him running out of her motel room, no shoes on and his chest bare, they might have thought he was running away from the scene of a murder.

Instead of towards a possible future murder.

Jolie didn't want anyone killed, but if that had to happen, she sent a selfish prayer to anyone listening that it wouldn't be him.

Jolie heard the howl in the distance as Liam crossed the two lane highway and vanished into the trees. God, he must have an excellent sense of hearing. It was a small miracle Red had managed to sneak up on them at all.

She grabbed her shoes, quickly stuffed her feet into them, and closed the door behind herself as she exited the motel room.

She felt guilty about leaving without paying—and the

broken television and door—just not guilty enough to stick around and let herself get caught.

There were only two vehicles parked in front of the motel, but it was enough to make Jolie glance around nervously for any sign someone might see her leaving.

She walked at first, trying to stay calm, trying not to draw any attention to herself. When she was a fair distance down the highway, but still within sight of the motel, that was when she started to run, needing to get as far away from the scene as she possibly could.

The running made her head hurt again. God, she should have taken one of her headache pills before leaving. Now that Liam wasn't on top of her and kissing her, the pain came back and throbbed behind her eyes and sinuses. It forced her to stop running sooner than she knew she was capable of running, if only to stop her brain from bouncing around like that inside her head.

She pulled the backpack off her shoulder, digging through it and yanking out the map. She ripped it a little, cursed at herself, angry as well as in pain.

What she wouldn't give to have a fully charged cell phone back in her possession.

This would have to do.

Another howl sounded in the distance.

Jolie clenched her jaw, opening the map as she walked, forcing herself not to look back.

He was going to be fine. Liam was an exceptional wolf, even for an alpha. He was strong. There was no way in hell Dempsey was going to get the better of him.

And if by some miracle he did, and Jolie found out about it, she was going to claw his eyes out.

She power walked for another two minutes before a red and gray wolf skidded in front of her, kicking up rocks on the side of the road.

Jolie stopped, took one look at them, then turned and walked in the other direction.

"Jolie, you can't just ignore us," Red called.

"Yes I can," she snapped back. Maybe if she was lucky, she could make it back to the motel. She could make up some kind of story and get the manager to call the police.

Well, actually, she wouldn't have to make up much of anything. She was alone on the side of the road and two men were following her. The cops would probably come for that.

"Jolie, come on, please just stop," Red called.

"Fuck off!" Jolie snapped.

It was Carl who had been with him, apparently. He rushed in front of Jolie, getting in her way. Jolie stopped, sighing. Red was definitely behind her, and now the two of them were boxing her in.

And she was fucking furious as she shoved her hand into her backpack.

"What are you reaching for?" Carl asked, his eyes turning gold.

"None of your damned business. Are you serious, Red? You came to scope us out and now you're here to pick me up while Liam is away?"

Red didn't sound happy about it, but she wasn't in the mood to feel any sympathy for him.

"It's not like that. We're just doing as we're told."

"Right, distracting Liam so you guys can pick me off." She glared over her shoulder at Red, and in that moment, she hated him. She really did.

"It could be worse," Red said, his shoulders hunched, his hands stuffed into the pockets of his jeans. "Dempsey was going to meet you down the road if you'd gone that way." He actually pointed down the road, as if she needed directions for the opposite end of the highway.

Still, she looked. "Are you serious?"

It didn't really shock her. She was more annoyed than shocked. And she swore that she was going to get back at Dempsey for this.

They'd known. Maybe they'd known if they made enough noise it would summon Liam to them. Even now she could hear the sounds of a wolf's howl.

"That's Dustin," said Red. "We're supposed to howl when we have you."

"And what happens to Liam?"

"Please get your hand out of the bag, Jolie," Carl said.

Jolie glared at him. He approached her. She didn't care.

"Carl, just give me a minute," Red said.

"She could have a gun in there for all you know." Carl reached out for Jolie's bag. "Let me see your hands! *Arghhhh!*"

Carl fell back, his hands flying to his eyes when she sprayed him. Bright red stained his cheeks and mouth when she over sprayed him, but she'd definitely gotten him in the eyes.

"Jesus! Jolie!" Red snapped.

Jolie didn't stop glaring down at Carl, and she was so furious that they would obey Renzo's and Dempsey's orders to bring her back that she kicked Carl in the gut when he was down and didn't feel an ounce of shame for it.

Carl seemed to barely feel the pressure from her foot as he squashed the heels of his palms into his eyes, as if that would take the pain away from him.

"You bitch! Oh fuck! Oh God, that hurts."

"Jolie," Red said. His hands grabbed hers before she could kick him again.

"It's supposed to hurt, you stupid asshole!"

She wanted to spray him again, to make sure he would be feeling the heat of the pepper spray for the next several days, but Red yanked the little bottle out of her hand, backing away from her with her weapon just as she swiped her small claws at his face.

He ducked back easily, looked at the bottle, and then at her.

And she glared at him. "Stop looking at me like that! You're the dickless asshole who wants me to mate with Dempsey!"

"I don't want you to mate with Dempsey," Red said. "It's Renzo's rule, and Dempsey will be my alpha one day."

"The way he commands you all now you'd think you were already his pack of bitches."

"Please don't be like that."

"Then swear your allegiance to Liam!"

Red tensed, his eyes flying wide as he stared down at where Carl was still on the ground, rolling and groaning in pain.

Jolie caught that look, and she glared at him. "What? Afraid someone will find out? How do you know I won't tell Renzo what you did if you take me in?"

"I'll tell him you lied, and you can't prove anything. When I bring you in, he'll believe me over you."

Jolie sneered at him. "You're pathetic."

The insult was weak, really, so she was stunned that it seemed to have an effect on him. As if she'd stabbed him through the ribs with a thin, rusty knife.

And that pained expression left his face quickly, replaced with an angry rage Jolie couldn't remember ever seeing on him before.

"I'm pathetic? Really? You know it's all well and good for you to run away and spite Renzo and Dempsey. You don't have anyone back at the pack waiting for you that they can hurt. I've got my mom and my sister."

"So you're going to sell me out?"

"For them? You're damn right," Red spat. "Are you out of

your fucking mind? Do you really think I would risk my family for you? That I would turn my back so you can go off and have your happily ever after with Liam while the rest of us were left to rot? How Goddamned selfish can you be?"

Jolie clenched her hands into fists. She hated him. So much. She hated Red for doing this to her and shaming her for wanting a better life for herself. And she hated him even more because it was working. She had forgotten about the people she was leaving behind. For the most part, anyway.

She'd thought it would be so easy if Liam made a play to take over the pack, that all he needed was for enough of the betas to swear their loyalty to him and Renzo would have no choice but to accept any challenge that came his way.

Right. Why would any of the betas switch sides when they all had families to take care of? Wives and children, siblings and parents.

Basically, anyone Renzo could use against them.

And in that moment, she knew she wouldn't rat Red out for so much as thinking of changing sides. Not when the risk was so high.

Red didn't stop glaring at her. He did snap his hand out, grabbing her around the wrist tight enough that the grip actually hurt.

Carl still groaned and hissed, the palms of his hands pressed hard into his eyes. "Oh God, you fucking bitch. Fuck! Jolie!"

"Shut up," Red snapped. "I have her. Let's just get out of here."

"I can barely see!"

"Which means you can see a little. Hurry up. The sooner we get out of here, the sooner we can wash your eyes out with some water." Red looked pointedly at Jolie. "You're not going to try anything again, are you?"

Jolie briefly bit her lips together. She shook her head.

Red nodded. "Good."

"Liam is going to come for me, you know that, right?"

In fact, it was such an obvious move from her mate that she had yet to feel any fear about being taken away, and ultimately, being forced to stand in front of Renzo again.

Red kept walking. He didn't look back at her, or question her, the way Jolie hoped he would. He just pulled her into the trees. Carl eventually followed behind, still cursing and calling Jolie all kinds of names as he hobbled along behind them.

As Red pulled her into the trees, presumably where he had a shortcut to the vehicle he'd driven here since she couldn't imagine anyone thinking she would willingly walk back to the pack, Jolie had to speak up again, just to make absolutely sure he could hear her.

"Liam will figure out pretty fast what you did, and when he does, he's going to be majorly pissed off at you."

The fact that Red was still avoiding looking back at her was a problem.

Jolie glanced behind her to Carl, who also averted his gaze, though he still looked angry, and squinty-eyed.

Their silence didn't speak well for Liam. It meant they knew something she did not, something that was sure as hell to make her panic if either of them said it out loud.

Rocks of ice filled her stomach, and Jolie couldn't help herself. She flew into a panic.

She yanked and pulled hard on her arm, forgoing being taken gracefully as she shrieked her head off. She had to get to him! She had to stop them! They were going to kill Liam!

She couldn't break the hold Red had on her wrist. The most she seemed to do was annoy him, even as she threw all of her bodyweight into struggling against him, into pulling away.

He reached back and wrapped his arms around hers,

pinning them to her sides. She turned her head and bit down as hard as she could on Red's bicep as he started to run with her. When a hand came over her mouth, she bit that too. Until she tasted blood.

Red hissed, yanking his hand back. Jolie started to scream again, desperate for anyone to hear her, even if it was just some humans who were taking a hike off the highway. She didn't care, she just wanted someone to hear her and stop this from happening.

Red and Carl scrambled. Another hand came down on her mouth. This time it was Carl's, doing his part to keep her calm and quiet while the both of them carted her off as if she was their latest kill.

She bit his hand, too, but he didn't pull back the way Red had, and when they made it to Red's truck, her heart sank.

Red threw her into the back. Carl jumped in with her as Red got into the driver's seat.

Jolie couldn't stop fighting. She couldn't stop herself from throwing punches at Carl's face. She wanted to hurt him as much as possible. She wanted to do permanent damage, scar his face, make him pay for what he was doing to her and make sure he never forgot it for the rest of his life.

The fact that she couldn't do the sort of damage she desperately wanted to do, that she was so helpless against him as he yanked her into his lap, curling one arm around her middle while his other hand came back up to her mouth, was infuriating enough that she almost cried.

"Bite me again, and I promise you're not getting back to Dempsey in one piece," Carl hissed.

Jolie had half a mind to bite him anyway just to see if he was serious about it.

"You're not going to do jack shit to her," Red snapped, putting the truck in gear and hitting the gas. They were off the road so it was a bumpy ride. "We're taking her home and you're just going to keep her quiet."

"She bites me and I'll make her wish she hadn't," Carl mumbled, as if to make sure she knew he would do something if she fought him back.

Jolie bit him anyway, enjoying the sound of his scream.

CHAPTER 15

She was brought back to the pack as if she was a runaway teenager.

Some people looked at her, as if they couldn't help but want to glance at what had become of her, only to swiftly turn their gazes elsewhere when they realized how awkward the situation was.

Jolie glared at the lot of them, searching for anyone's eyes and daring them all to at least look at her. After a while, no one did. That was fine; it was a short walk through the pack and up the deck stairs of Renzo's house.

Carl left them as soon as they made it back. It only took two hours of driving. Jolie was upset with herself, even as Red knocked on the front door.

She'd known that she and Liam hadn't made it that far out on foot, but the fact that it was only a two hour drive?

Her fault. Her fault for not being able to handle the elements when in her wolf form, her fault for not knowing how to hunt and making Liam feel as if he needed to teach her.

It was entirely her fault.

"Jolie, I'm really sorry," Red said, his voice low. His hand still held her arm tight enough that she wouldn't be able to get away, but his grip wasn't as tight as it had been before.

It still felt as if there was an iron shackle on her skin.

The door opened. Renzo was there, not the omega who usually cleaned up after him, and one look at Jolie and his jaw tightened.

"Not happy to see me?" Jolie asked.

Renzo rolled his shoulders. His long salt-and-pepper hair was out of its usual ponytail. There were slight bags under his eyes. "Yes, well, you've caused a lot of trouble lately. Get in here, the both of you."

He said it as if Jolie could opt out of that, but Red pushed her inside, staying close to her back, and still holding her as if he thought she was going to bolt at any moment.

She would. The second he let her go, she would leap into action and, if she had to, make a hole through one of the walls in the perfect shape of her body. Old cartoon style.

Renzo brought them to the living room. He pointed to the couch. "Sit."

Red didn't move right away. "Do you want me to leave you alone, sir?"

"No, you too," Renzo said.

Jolie's brows lifted up high. Okay. What did he want with Red?

Red looked down at her. She could see the glint of panic in his eyes. She even wanted to tell him that she hadn't told anyone else that he'd paid her and Liam a visit yesterday, but along with giving him away, she supposed he wouldn't believe her anyway.

If Renzo did know about it, how had he found out?

Red didn't question his alpha a second time. He just did as he was told, holding much tighter to Jolie's arm than he had been just a second ago. He walked stiffly, and sat down awkwardly with her.

Jolie was starting to feel sorrier for him in this situation.

Renzo *knew*. He had to know. And now he was playing with Red.

Renzo grabbed himself a bottle of water from the mini-fridge in the corner. He twisted the cap off, took a leisurely drink, and stared out the window in front of him as the people outside hurried along, either on the way to their jobs, or to get their chores around the pack finished up.

He acted as if he didn't have a runaway omega and potential traitor in his house.

"I guess Dempsey didn't come back?" Jolie asked.

If she didn't say anything then Red's terror was going to latch onto her like the contagious disease that it was. She wouldn't be able to stop herself from freaking out if that happened.

Renzo didn't turn back to look at her. "Not yet. I got a call from him when he finished with Liam."

Jolie's heart did a flip, and then landed wrong and broke both of its legs.

From the corner of her eye, she caught the way Red looked at her.

"Finished with him?"

Renzo finally spun around, his smile as pleasant as if they were talking about the vegetable patch outside, instead of insinuating murder.

"Jolie, he was a wild wolf. He has been ever since he killed Dempsey's father."

"He was defending his mother," Jolie said, her fingers digging into her jeans.

"And he had no right to kill Dougal, no matter the circumstances. That is a decision for an alpha to make."

"A decision you were never going to make, because you're a coward and the worst alpha to walk the face of the earth."

He didn't seem nearly as hurt by her words as she wanted him to be. Renzo just came to sit down in the reading chair across from her and Red on the other side of the glass coffee table. He just...looked at her, his expression confident, sure, and giving away no hints that he thought he'd done a damned thing wrong.

Jolie snapped. "He's not dead! Liam is alive and he's coming for me, you asshole! I'll die before I ever let Dempsey mate with me!"

Once again, the lack of response from Renzo made the frustration and pain seem so much worse. She couldn't describe it. The anger and hate boiling inside her was unlike anything she'd ever felt before in her life.

She'd never really liked Renzo. After Liam's parents died and he was exiled, Renzo was just the alpha. Someone who ruled the pack, strict, but didn't stir things up too much.

Now, she despised him, and God, what she would give to be able to melt his face with her stare right about now.

"Why won't you just be Dempsey's mate?"

Jolie blinked. "What?"

"His mate," Renzo said again. "I understand Liam was your childhood friend—"

"Stop saying *was*!"

"But Dempsey will be a good alpha one day when I retire. Or when he fights me for it." Renzo smiled. "I hope he fights me for it, that's the way of a true man, and even if he doesn't fight me for control of the pack," he said, as if *not* fighting and risking his and Dempsey's deaths in the process was a terrible thing to consider, "then he would still make a good mate for you. He would give you healthy pups, see to it you were sheltered and fed. I don't think he would be the type to hit you. At the very least, he wouldn't do it often."

"Great," Jolie deadpanned.

Renzo shook his head. "It's not a healthy thing for an omega to be so picky in her choice of mate."

"It's not my choice and I'm not mating with him!"

For the first time, Renzo finally showed some hint that he was getting annoyed with her attitude.

Jolie yanked her arm away from Red. He let her go. She leaned back on the couch and crossed her arms. "You can't make me mate with Dempsey."

"And if Liam is dead?" Renzo asked. "You'll be alone and destitute. No one will take you in this time around. I'll see to that."

She hated him. She hated him so much, but she used that rush of bravery she felt within herself to keep on going, because Liam was absolutely *not* dead. She just had to wait this out. Wait for him to get here, or for an opening to present itself so she could get out of there.

Liam had been trying to teach her how to hunt for a reason beyond keeping fed. He'd wanted to know she could handle herself if he ever wasn't around for her.

She had every intention of making him proud.

"Don't have much of an answer for that one, do you?"

"If Liam is dead, and that's a big *if*," she said, "then I'll get out of this stupid pack and get a job. You know, like an adult."

"You won't be able to leave," Renzo said. "That's not for you to decide."

"Fine, then I'll just escape when you're not looking."

"And I will have you picked up again," Renzo said. His eyes softened. "Don't make me force this on you."

"*Make you?*" Jolie jumped to her feet. She couldn't stay sitting when he said such a horrifyingly stupid thing to her. "You're going to act all sorry while talking about letting Dempsey rape me? Are you kidding? What's the *matter* with you?"

"You would be his mate. It would hardly be rape." He sneered at her. "Don't accuse me of such despicable things."

Jolie couldn't tell if he was purposely missing the point or not, and that was definitely a little worrisome.

"You won't let me leave, you won't accept that I'm mated to Liam—"

"Even if you were mated to that wild mutt, he's dead now, so there's no point in arguing over it." Again with that pitying expression, as if he was sorry to be arguing with her over this at all. "Just take the offer for a mate and be done with it. You will be kept comfortable. You will be fed and clothed and protected. I'm tired. I don't want to have this argument again and again."

Ah, so that was it. Her answer was right there. He wasn't sorry for the way he was treating her, he was sorry that he had to go through the trouble at all.

"Can't Dempsey just find someone else? There's literally nothing all that special about me."

"Well, I suppose I *could* command Red's sister to mate with Dempsey if you really didn't want to."

Jolie tensed. Red choked behind her. She didn't look back at him.

And Renzo smirked at her, as if to say he finally had her. "Yes, you see? I do have other alternatives."

"But..." Jolie couldn't think of what to say just then. She was completely and totally tongue-tied.

Not a good feeling to have when Renzo was looking at her like that.

She recovered. "What the fuck is going on? Are you seriously saying that Dempsey can't find a mate on his own that you have to force him onto other people?"

Much as she didn't want to admit it, Dempsey wasn't an ugly guy. In fact, he was fairly good-looking. He shouldn't have had any trouble at all finding a mate for himself. It would probably have to be outside of the pack since there were very few women in this one willing to overlook the cruel holier-than-thou attitude he brought to absolutely everything.

"Just you, it seems," Renzo replied. "I don't want it to come down to that, and neither does he, but I will arrange to have it done if you insist on fighting me every step of the way."

Jolie turned back to look at Red. He was still sitting on the couch, his hands on his knees, and his face a pale grey color.

He looked like death.

"Look," Renzo started, commanding her attention once more. "I don't know what he sees in you. Personally, if I had been chasing down an omega, whether it was for some tail, or something more long-term, if she had rebuffed me every step of the way, at some point, I would have taken the hint."

"But not for me."

"Well, that's on him, not me," Renzo replied. He took another swig of his water, then glanced down at the bottle, shaking his head. "I need something stronger than this." He got to his feet, walking over to the decanter in the glass cabinet. He poured himself a drink.

"So because Dempsey wants me, I get no choice in it? Why can't you just tell him no?"

"Why can't you just tell him yes?" Renzo shot back.

That boiling anger rushed up inside her body one more time. Anymore and she was going to fly apart at the seams.

"He likes you. He begged for you for long enough, and he won't have anyone else." Renzo looked her in the eyes, his expression still cold, but there was something a little closer to human there now. "I tried to talk him out of it, but he wouldn't have it. He's convinced you're his destined mate, and if that's the case then I'm not about to get in the way of that."

"I'm not his destined mate!" Jolie clung to that piece of information. "I'm Liam's destined mate!"

"Why? Because he *told* you so?" Renzo snorted. "Please, as if I would take the word of that disease-ridden stray."

"Stop talking about him like that!" Jolie's body actually trembled. She couldn't stop it. Couldn't stop the hateful energy rushing through her. "He's not disease-ridden, a mutt, or a stray. He *has* a pack."

"Who? You alone?"

Jolie narrowed her eyes. "Yes. That's all he needs."

"Uh huh." Renzo looked anything but impressed. "I've tried to be patient with you. Don't you ever look back on this and try saying that I didn't, but I've made my decision."

"And I get to make no decision."

"Stop that. Dempsey is a fine young man and you're acting as if I was handing you over to Ted Bundy."

"It's the fact that you think you can hand me over to anyone at all that bugs me the most."

"Either way, it's done," Renzo insisted. "Liam is gone now. Dempsey confirmed it. You are without a mate and the future alpha of this pack wants you by his side. No more arguments. I'm not going to have the mate of the future alpha behaving like a spoiled brat."

Jolie barely heard a word after Renzo said *confirmed*.

Confirmed? As in someone had called him and told him flat out that Liam was…dead?

That terror-stricken panic took hold of her heart once more, and it was sure as hell hard for her to pretend to be confident about anything when Renzo spoke like that.

"Jolie! Hey, snap out of it." Renzo actually snapped his fingers in front of her face, and that was all she needed to be yanked out of the trance she was in.

And Renzo was right there, looking at her as if he had no idea he'd just devastated her. Or as if he didn't care that was what he was doing.

Jolie shook her head. "He's not dead. They didn't kill him."

She would have *felt* it. She was sure of it. That was the point of being mated. To have that connection to another person, to trust and love someone so completely and totally that her senses were consumed by it. If Liam's soul had left the Earth, then Jolie would have known about it. Her spirit would have registered the loss. She was sure of it.

Renzo crossed his arms. "Dempsey called me and gave me the news himself. It's for the best. He was living in squalor that entire time and there's no telling how it could have affected his mind, or what it made him want to do. You and the rest of the pack are far safer now that—"

Renzo stopped abruptly. He didn't scream, but he did jerk his body back hard and fast when Jolie's claws came out as she reached out for his eyes. Just as Liam had told her to do if she was ever backed into a corner.

She wasn't about to let him get away. As she flew forward, he fell back, the instinct to protect his eyes too strong for an alpha to ignore, even when the threat was coming from a weak little omega, it seemed.

He fell backwards into the coffee table. The glass shattered into a thousand glittering pieces both large and small. It was dangerous, but Jolie wanted to go down with him, roll around in the glass and make sure she sliced his face and body everywhere that she could. She had the alpha on the ground in front of her, who cared if she was cut up a little by the glass, or if he was trying to get to his feet so he could properly defend himself?

Red wouldn't let her. He grabbed her just as she fell onto

Renzo, before she could slam his head down into the broken glass, and he yanked her clean off her feet.

"Whoa! Jolie! *Knock it off!*"

She ignored him. Jolie hardly heard a word Red said after that as she screeched like a wild animal, her small claws and teeth out, red hot revenge clouding her judgement as she struggled to go up against a creature that was way more powerful than she would ever be.

Renzo calmly pushed himself to his feet, glanced beneath him to the broken glass, and the fact that there was no blood on him made Jolie go that much wilder as she desperately struck her claws out again and again.

The hard smack across her face slapped the wild animal out of her mind. Jolie's entire body stopped. She paused, breathed, then looked back at the alpha.

Renzo lifted a single dark brow as he looked at her. "Don't know whether to beat some sense into you or be proud of you. I'll figure that one out later." He nodded to Red. "Take her to my guest room, and then you and I are going to have a little talk."

Jolie felt the throb of Red's heart against her back. Yeah, he was in trouble, and he knew it.

"Yes, alpha," Red said, his voice wobbling only slightly as he carried Jolie towards the guest room. One of the room's Jolie had stayed in as a child when she'd lived here with Liam.

Before her rightful alpha had been killed and Renzo took over.

Red put her onto her feet in the bedroom. It was obvious just from looking around how it had been prepared for her. Pretty much anything had been stripped out of the room that could be used as a weapon, or broken and made into one, with the exception of the glass window.

And she didn't think she'd get very far if she tried smashing it.

"Let me guess, there's someone outside my window making sure I don't try to leave?"

"Probably," Red said. "Just don't cause any trouble, *please*."

Jolie looked at the man, and she looked hard. Red seemed to have trouble holding her gaze, but that wasn't Jolie's problem. In that moment, it felt as if she was looking right through him. And she felt something for him she'd promised herself she wouldn't feel when he took her off the side of the road.

Pity.

"I don't know when Renzo turned into a complete dictator, or if he always was and I just never noticed, but Liam *is* coming back."

Red made a pained face. "Jolie."

"And I don't care if Renzo is listening to this. I hope he is listening," Jolie snapped, letting her voice get louder and louder with every word she spoke. She looked passed Red and down the hall, as if Renzo was standing right there, because she knew he could hear her. "Because when Liam gets here, he's going to kick Renzo's ass and take back his pack that Renzo stole from him, and I'll be cheering him on the entire time."

Jolie returned her heated glare to Red. His eyes were so wide she could see the whites all the way around the blues.

"So when he gets here, you, and everyone else who's sick of Renzo's bullshit, better make a decision about who you would rather follow, and you'd better make it fast."

As if to accent her words, a howl sounded in the distance. Jolie's wolf ears had popped out without her even noticing, though they flicked at the noise.

The familiar noise of her mate.

She smiled.

CHAPTER 16

The wolf's howl was more than enough to let her know he was coming. Of course he was. Liam was absolutely not dead, and she had no idea how he'd managed to make Dempsey call in and say he was, but she didn't care.

The sound of the howl made her want to shift and howl back. All the fear she'd been harbouring inside her ever since Red and Carl had taken her from the side of the road melted away, and she wanted to fight again.

That was a big one. She'd never wanted to jump into a battle so badly before. She'd always gone out of her way to avoid them, but then she'd attacked Renzo, and now she couldn't stop pacing around the room she'd been shoved in.

Red had locked the door after leaving her, and she'd been right earlier on when she'd asked if there was someone posted outside the window to make sure she didn't start any trouble. Patrick was beneath her window, and he, along with everyone else she could see from her view, were on high alert at the sound of that howl.

Her ears twitched as she heard it again. Renzo yelled and cursed at Red in the house, but her entire focus was on the swan song of that howl. Her heart pulled at the next long call. Goosebumps rose along her skin as every small hair on her body stood on end.

The inner wild side Jolie didn't even know she had was on high alert. She wanted to open the window, to put as little between herself and that noise as possible.

She wanted, *needed*, to howl back. She didn't know why, and even though she felt kind of silly for it, she had to do it.

Jolie went to the window. Of course it was locked. From the outside. She only noticed the padlock on the outside of the window after a bit of searching.

Patrick heard her struggling with the window. He turned back to look at her.

She ignored him. The only way she would be getting the window open would be if she smashed the glass.

Liam howled again, howled for her. She felt it now. She knew what he wanted. He was waiting for her to answer him. He'd been waiting all this time, and now that she knew it, she couldn't contain herself. She had to answer his call. Had to let him know she was here, waiting for him.

As if her howl was a living, breathing thing that needed to be released from her body, Jolie clutched at her arms, as if to keep herself from flying apart with the heat swelling within her.

Raw instinct. Something she'd never before felt in her life as an omega.

She threw her head back and howled at the ceiling. The noise was amplified. She howled again, louder, her inner wolf coming out, both of them howling together, howling for their mate.

And it was as if a great pressure was being released from her body. As if Liam's hands were on her skin in that moment, sliding along her shoulders, the warmth of his breath ghosting along her exposed throat, his voice in her ear, low, rumbling, pleased.

"I'm coming."

Another ripple of pleasure and goosebumps washed over her like a wave.

She knew. She *knew* he was coming, knew he could hear her, even though she was confined in this stupid room. She howled louder.

Was this what Liam felt when he'd lived for so many years as a wild wolf? Without his mate? This intense pressure? This heat and longing that refused to be satisfied without him?

She'd thought she'd known what it felt like. Jolie wrongly assumed she had any sort of clue about it when she finally found him. That longing had only been a taste of what this was. This was real instinct. This was real longing, and Dempsey was out of his damned mind if he thought there was any universe where she would feel this way for him.

Renzo's booming scream on the other side of the door knocked her out of her wolfy trance. She spun around, just as the door exploded inward as Renzo broke it down.

As if he didn't have the ability to just unlock it.

He stomped forward, his eyes blazing red, his hand stroking out, fingers and claws gripping tightly to her throat. He yanked her forward, showing off his teeth as he hissed in her face. "Stop *howling*."

Jolie glared at him. She swiped her claws at his face. He was faster, catching her wrist and gripping hard enough that she screamed the last of the air in her lungs.

A small snapping sent a huge shockwave up her arm. Renzo dropped her, and she couldn't catch herself. She fell to her side, clutching at her arm.

Renzo breathed hard above her, his chest heaving, fists clenched as he shook his head. "Jesus Christ, fine! Enough."

He reached down, grabbing a fistful of Jolie's hair, yanking her to her feet.

She groaned, her wobbling legs struggling to keep up, or else she was about to gain a fairly large bald spot on top of her head.

Renzo hardly seemed to notice how he hurt her as he dragged her out of the spare room. She could hardly keep up, or stay on her feet. "If you want to go live in the woods with a wild mutt then *fine*. Never knew what Dempsey saw in you anyway."

He ranted continuously as he pulled her down the hall. Even when Jolie managed to get to her feet, she was forced to keep walking bent over.

Carl and Dustin rushed to the steps of the deck just as Renzo exited the home he'd stolen from Liam.

Jolie could only just barely glance up at them from her current position. Concerned was too mild a word for what was on their faces. Dustin's voice actually trembled. "Alpha! Liam's coming! He has Dempsey."

"What happened to the betas sent with him?"

Jolie's heart skipped, but in the best way possible. She had an idea of what happened to the betas, but she wasn't about to say it out loud to Renzo. Not when she was in such a vulnerable position, at any rate.

Dustin's worried expression changed, as if he was just asked a question he had no idea how to answer. He and Carl looked at each other, and the sentiment was clearly the same for Carl.

"Well?" Renzo snapped. "Out with it! He couldn't have killed them all!"

Omegas and betas who were doing their chores and going about their business took note of what was happening on the deck. They stopped to watch. Some spoke softly to each other, as if they couldn't believe this was happening.

Or that it had taken so long for this to come to a head.

"Well, uh..." Carl stammered.

"They kind of..." Dustin actually rubbed at his wrist, the both of them completely tongue-tied.

Chatter started up suddenly, and people started to move. It took Jolie a second to notice with the way she was positioned, but when she did, the flow of people had picked up, and it seemed they were all heading in the same direction.

Towards the road coming onto pack property.

No one got too close. They seemed to form a half circle around as the group walked onto the property, and even when it looked as if they got as close as they were going to get, the people parted like the red sea.

It was a magnificent sight, even as she was looking at it bent over the way she was.

Liam looked like a dirty, sweaty, muscular warrior who had just come victorious from a battle. Five betas walked behind him like the flying V she sometimes saw birds do in the sky.

Every muscle in his arms, legs, and shoulders was tense, his hands clenched into fists. Even with the dry mud smeared on his body, she could not only see the ferocity on him, but she also felt it swirling around him like a dark aura, and that was despite the distance.

"Motherfucker," Renzo cursed softly.

Dempsey was at the very back of Liam's men, being dragged along, his hands tied behind him, though Jolie couldn't see with what.

The only thing she kept her eyes on was Liam, and the closer he got, the easier it was to see the whites of his fangs as he stormed forward.

No one, not even the other betas in the pack, stepped in his way as he stomped naked up to the steps of the deck.

"That's as far as you go," Renzo snapped.

Liam stopped. At first, his obedience shocked her, but then she realized that it wasn't obedience. Renzo had Liam's mate in his grasp. That would be enough to make any decent alpha stop in his tracks.

"I want her back," Liam said. "We can trade."

He didn't specify what, but it was clear he was talking about Dempsey. Now that they were standing so close, Jolie could see Dempsey was gagged with a belt. He was probably tied up with one as well. His eyes were swollen in the early stages of bruising. Blood dribbled from his nose, mouth, and made a red trail down his chin.

Liam had done a number on him.

Renzo didn't answer right away; that was concerning.

Liam's eyes flashed red. He growled shortly, but turned his attention to Jolie. "Did he hurt you?"

"Just my back from being in this position for so long," she said, purposely groaning her words and elbowing Renzo in the leg for good measure.

Renzo didn't give any indication that her petty strike had hurt him, but he did growl and yank her up to a more upright position. He pulled her by her hair in order to do it, but the pain trade off from her head was worth it considering how much better her back felt.

Still, she glared at Renzo. "Thanks." She smiled for Liam. "I'm fine. Thanks for coming for me."

"Wouldn't have left you behind for a thing," he growled, his heated glare still working hard at burning that hole through Renzo's forehead.

Jolie's heart swelled painfully hard before it started beating again. Liquid happiness was injected right into her vein with those words.

She'd only been separated from him for a couple of hours, but now that he was in front of her again, something inside her was set free and wild.

Maybe she'd been a little more worried than she'd let herself believe, because now that he was here, it felt as if she could only now really start to breathe. As if she was going to be all right.

"I said I want to trade." Liam snapped his fingers. The betas in the very back, Josh and Franky, pulled Dempsey forward, then kicked his legs out behind him so he was on his knees next to Liam.

The entire pack watched with rapt attention. No one could seem to look away from the mess happening in front of them. It was as if the entire pack, the men, women and pups, were in a trance.

It even took Renzo a minute before he was able to think of something to say. "Did he really scare you so much that you all had to follow this wild animal?"

The betas behind Liam kept their backs straight. They showed no sign of weakness, no shifting from foot to foot, no glancing nervously at each other. They looked like a unit, like a team of betas who were loyal to their alpha, and would follow him through a raging fire if he commanded it.

And the pride that had been swelling within Jolie's chest went to level nine thousand. She's suspected it the second she realized what had happened, but this was all the confirmation she needed.

Liam hadn't threatened them into helping him. They weren't behind him because they were fearful of what he might do to Dempsey either. They stood behind him as a proud unit because they had clearly seen his strength in action; only unlike Red, they didn't seem to need much more proof about his strength as a leader.

Jolie had no idea of the details involved with their decision to abandon Dempsey and look to Liam as their alpha, and she didn't care. The only thing she cared about was the decision had been made at all.

A real alpha had come along, and now they were going to fall in line.

Renzo made a disgusted noise when none of the betas answered him.

"Pathetic, and weak, the lot of you," he sneered.

Dempsey tried to speak through his gag, but it just came out as garbled gibberish with the belt in his mouth.

Jolie tensed when something prickled the back of her head. She knew it was Renzo's claws, and the happy, joyous excitement that rushed through her when Liam marched through the pack as if he owned the place was replaced with the worry she never should have stopped feeling.

"You gonna let my boy talk, or do I have to get messy on your little girl here?"

Jolie swallowed. She was too nervous to even be all that insulted by the *little girl* remark.

Would he actually do it? Would he hurt an omega just to keep a challenging alpha at bay?

She didn't know. She had absolutely no idea what to expect and that was the worst thing possible. Despite living under his rule for so many years, Renzo had been too closed off, too hard to read. He'd taken care of the pack well enough over the years, but there was no telling if he'd secretly been hiding something much darker beneath his strict veneer.

The claws at the back of her head certainly suggested he was willing to go down a darker path than simply killing an alpha during a supremacy fight.

Liam clearly realized what Renzo was doing. It must have been all over Jolie's face.

"You would threaten an omega?"

"You're threatening my position and the young man who's practically my son. It evens out," Renzo deadpanned.

"Then make the trade," Liam growled. "My mate for this sack of shit. Then I will go and not come back."

"Uh huh, and what will you be doing with those betas?"

Liam didn't so much as glance behind him. "They can do what they want. I won't stop them."

Wait a minute? What? This wasn't how it was supposed to go down. He was supposed to fight for the pack now. Take over and kick Renzo, Dempsey, and anyone who still supported them out.

"Right, somehow I doubt they'll be sticking around for what I'll have in store for betraying the pack."

"Then next time send a better representative of it," Liam said, and he kicked Dempsey in the back, forcing him to fall forward on his chest, unable to catch himself. The man coughed helplessly in the dirt. "Your betas witnessed a powerful alpha dominating the little bitch they were following. I can hardly blame them for wanting to follow me in his place. Or yours."

Renzo growled. "I think you're forgetting what I have here."

"And you just confirmed you think of Dempsey as a son. The son you never had. It's a shame I never killed you instead of his father. I might try to rectify that now if you don't make the trade." Liam's eyes were such a bright shade of red that they positively glowed.

Jolie didn't have to look at Renzo to know his eyes were a mirror image.

"Gah!" Jolie let out a hard shriek as the world tilted on her. Out of control, she fell down the stairs after Renzo, pushed hard against the back of her head.

Liam stepped forward, catching her before she could land on her face the same way Dempsey had after he'd been shoved. Landing in his arms, no matter how preferred it was, still knocked the wind out of her.

Jolie groaned as Liam backed away, her toes barely touching the ground. He pretty much had to drag her away from Renzo, never taking his eyes off the alpha, putting distance between the two of them and Renzo's cabin.

"Anyone tries to follow, and I won't be as kind as I was to your adopted fuck up."

"Just get off my property," Renzo growled. "Five stupid betas still aren't enough to go against me and every other beta still loyal to me. I've been running this pack smoothly for years. You have zero claim to it."

Liam growled, but he didn't reply. Jolie held out a small hope that he would, some tiny hint that he wanted to remove Renzo from his position, but he said nothing.

"Red! Move your ass. Get Dempsey to his feet and inside."

Jolie turned her attention to Red, just as the man rushed to do as he was told. Not only him, but a couple of other betas, as well, who quickly untied Dempsey's arms and helped him to his feet.

The way Dempsey growled and groaned, clenching his teeth and hissing in pain as he was walked up the stairs of the deck, indicated that his wounds were much more than just shallow. Liam had done some real damage to him.

And as the betas helped him up the stairs, and as Renzo and Liam glared at each other, Red glanced back.

Another hope. Another soft wish that something else would go her way, that Red would come to his senses, fly down those stairs, rush over to Liam to declare his loyalty and wish to serve the rightful alpha of the pack, even if it meant having to leave it.

Red quickly turned away from them, his attention back to Dempsey as he did as he was told.

Jolie deflated. Right. Red still had his family to think about. He wouldn't be joining them as they left.

Liam continued to back up, never taking his eyes away from Renzo, but she also got the feeling he was keeping his attention on the rest of the pack as well.

And he was right to. Jolie could breathe properly again instead of wheezing, thank God, but when that was out of the way and she noted what was going on around her, it was easy to see the beta males stepping forward, as if they would spring on her, Liam, and the five betas he'd converted if given the opportunity.

Or the command.

"Liam," Jolie said, her voice coming out smaller than she meant it to.

"I see them," he said softly.

Renzo marched down the stairs of his deck, actually waving his fist like a crazed old man. "I'm warning you! Don't you ever come back here again! You hear me? And none of you traitorous bitches better dare show your faces either or I'll skin you all alive!"

Jolie shivered. She was pretty sure he didn't mean that literally, but it was hard to tell anything anymore.

At a certain point, Liam must have judged them to be far enough away that he could safely turn his back and make a run for it, which was exactly what he and the five betas did.

Jolie held on tightly as the wind rushed through her hair as, for the second time, she fled the only home she'd ever known.

CHAPTER 17

Jolie hissed as Liam ran with her. He was fast. Stupidly fast. No human would ever be able to keep up with him. As he flew through the trees, the betas running behind him, hardly able to keep up with him, she got the feeling an alpha would have trouble catching him, too.

The problem was the way she bounced in his arms. His tight grip on her body hurt, and at one point, she bit her tongue.

"You never told me you were so fast," she said, trying to smile about the whole thing, but then winced when she accidentally bit her tongue again.

Maybe it was best if she didn't say anything at all.

"Sorry, just hold on, we're going to be running for just a little while longer."

He looked, and sounded, as if he could be running until he reached the edge of the Earth. He wasn't so much as out of breath.

When he said they would only be running for a little while longer, he apparently meant it. Within another ten minutes or so of fast paced, Olympic worthy running, they made it to a clearing in the trees.

There were two sleek-looking SUVs ready and waiting for them. They were definitely Renzo's, and possibly Dempsey's, property.

Liam set her down on her feet when he came to a stop. The ground swirled beneath her just a little, and she had to reach out and grab onto Liam's arm just to make sure she could stand up straight without getting knocked on her ass.

Liam's hand came around her waist. He didn't say anything. He seemed to be back in one of his quiet moods, but the small touch warmed her from the inside out. She didn't need proof that he cared, or that he loved her, but the protective gesture, no matter how small, was more than welcome even after he'd rescued her.

"Josh, you're driving," Liam ordered, walking with Jolie to the passenger side of the first SUV.

"Anywhere special that we're going?"

Liam yanked open the door. "Anywhere so long as it puts a roof over my mate's head and isn't too far away. Even a campground will do. Just make it happen. You will all follow us," Liam commanded.

The other four betas nodded, and everyone separated out between vehicles. Franky climbed into the front passenger seat with Josh, while Peter and the other two went into the other SUV.

"Come on," Liam said, his large hands on Jolie's waist as he helped her up into the seat. She shifted over to the side, giving Liam room to sit next to her.

He shut the door. "Let's go," he commanded.

Josh did as he was told, starting the engine. It purred to life beneath them. These were definitely Renzo's babies. Jolie had never even been in these vehicles before, and with the leather seat beneath her, and the buttons and dials in front of her, she could kind of understand why.

The pack had always known Renzo had been over taxing them. It had been proven well enough when Renzo had purchased these vehicles to begin with, but to be inside and see everything…it was nuts.

"I don't like being driven," Liam growled, his hand reaching out and finding hers. Without so much as looking at her, he threaded their fingers together. "But it was the fastest way to get to you."

Jolie's heart wouldn't stop pounding. It was almost as if she had been the one making that epic run away from the pack instead of him. She was out of breath and honestly felt as if she was going to collapse at any moment.

Good thing she was still seated.

Liam finally looked at her. "Are you sure you're not hurt? When Renzo threw you—"

"I'm fine," she said quickly, managing to get her voice to work. "I'm just glad you came for me."

Liam's eyes flashed briefly to red before he got control over himself and the color changed back to normal. "I would always come for you." He glared up at the front seat. At first Jolie thought his glare was for Josh, but that wasn't the case. "I'm going to have to learn how to drive one of these soon. I don't like having someone else do it for us. I don't like relying on them."

Jolie blinked up at him, but it was easy to smile after that. She leaned against his arm. She didn't even mind that he was dirty. She kind of liked that about him. Proof of his hard work and efforts. Proof that he loved her enough to fight for her.

"They're your betas now. They won't disappoint you, will you, guys?" she asked, catching Josh's eyes briefly in the rearview mirror.

"No, Jolie. We saw what happened to Dempsey."

Franky turned in his chair to look at them, but his smile seemed mostly directed at Jolie. "It was scary as all hell, but kind of amazing. I don't think I ever saw even Renzo or Dempsey wolf out like that. It just sort of compels you to obey, you know?"

Jolie nodded. "Yeah, I know."

And she was beyond thrilled that Josh and Franky looked happy to be here. She was sure the same was true for Peter and the two others following behind them as they drove down the path.

Eventually, Josh turned onto an actual paved road, and Jolie sighed, finally feeling as if she'd hit civilization with a smoother ride.

And Franky wouldn't stop talking. "It was great. God, I wish I'd had my phone out so I could have recorded it. Dempsey was puffing his chest out, being a smug prick as usual, talking shit, and Liam wouldn't even let him finish his stupid speech about beating him down before Liam punches him in the face! It was amazing! Dempsey just stared at Liam like he didn't know what the fuck happened! He—uh, wait."

Franky's excitement turned to confusion, and then a touch of hurt as a black window slowly lifted, separating him and the entire front seat from Liam and Jolie.

Jolie looked at the black glass when it was entirely blocking the view. She leaned in close. She could make out what was happening in the front seat, but as Franky looked in the back, he didn't seem to see her at all.

"Tinted glass, huh?" she asked. "That was kind of mean."

"Yes, well, I don't like it when they start getting their dicks hard over how I beat the hell out of Dempsey."

"They're betas. They reacted to your strength. You're not only the son of their original alpha, but you're strong, too.

They remember you before you were kicked out of the pack. They're glad to have you here."

"I guess, so long as no other alpha comes along who's stronger than I am, they'll be my best friends until the end of time." Liam looked down at her.

Jolie squeezed his hand tighter. She looked at his knuckles. There was some dried blood on them. Not a lot. It could belong to either him or Dempsey, but it did symbolize the hurt and pain he'd gone through, not just to get her back, but throughout his entire life.

"You still don't trust them?" she asked, already knowing the answer.

Liam sighed. "You're disappointed."

Jolie quickly shook her head. "Not in the least, but I do know that the relationships alphas have with the betas, omegas, and even a few other alphas beneath them tend to be…complicated. I'm just glad they want to follow you, for however long you want to keep them. If they can help us, then that's all that matters."

"Right. If they'd had wives and children, they wouldn't have followed me for a second."

"No, but they do have parents and siblings." Jolie Liam in the eyes. "I don't think it was entirely about instinct. They made a decision to leave everything behind for you. For us. I'm grateful to them for that."

"I would have come for you even if they didn't want me to be their alpha," he said sharply. "I want you to know that."

And she *did* know it. Jolie nodded. "Yeah, I know." She stroked her hand over his bruised and bloody knuckles, and just because she had to, she brought his hand to her mouth, kissing his knuckles.

As if that would have made the sting he surely felt there go away.

It was the thought that counted, she hoped, at least.

"I love you. I know you would have come for me, and I know this isn't what you wanted. To have betas following you around, or a small pack, but I am glad they were there for you to make it easier to walk into the territory and throw Dempsey down." She couldn't help but grin widely. "I'm never going to forget how he looked when he fell on his face in the dirt."

Liam grinned back at her. She didn't often see him smile, so this time around seemed extra special. "It was nice, wasn't it?"

"He totally deserved it, and God, it feels good just thinking about it."

"I'll have to do it again when I go back."

That made her freeze. She looked at him, and she couldn't help but wonder if she'd actually heard that right.

Liam continued to look at her, as if he was waiting for a response.

Jolie had to shake herself out of her shock. "Wait, you're going back?"

He nodded. "I am."

Jolie blinked. "But…I thought you didn't want to fight for the pack? You were just going to leave it to Renzo."

"I was," he said, another nod, and then his eyes changed to a bright red. "But that was before I saw his hands on you. Now, I wouldn't mind liberating him of all the blood in his body."

The violence aside, Jolie was thrilled. She squealed a hard, high-pitched noise before throwing her arms around Liam's neck and clinging tight. Her mouth found his lips and cheeks, and then his lips again because she absolutely could not contain the rush of happiness that bubbled through her.

"All right, all right," Liam said. His hands went back to her waist, as though he was going to push her off. He didn't. He didn't even turn his head enough to avoid her kisses.

Which definitely meant he was letting his pride get in the way and secretly wanted more, so that was exactly what she gave to him.

Another hard kiss, more of a smack against his lips before she pulled back, feeling wide-eyed and full of energy. "You're going to take the pack back?"

"Yes," he said. His eyes were half-lidded. His gaze fell to her mouth. It wasn't lost on her that a slight pinkish sort of color had settled on his cheeks.

And his hands were still on her hips.

"I would do it for you, and for everyone else who does not want to be under Renzo's rule anymore but can't say no."

Red came to mind. Jolie got the feeling that Liam was thinking about the beta was well.

And Red was definitely not the only one. If he had been thinking about it but couldn't make the leap, then it wasn't a stretch to realize there were others who were sick of having Renzo in charge, too.

"Thank you," Jolie said. "Though I hope you won't have to kill anyone, somehow I doubt Renzo will just bow down and present his neck to you."

"No," Liam said, and then growled. "He won't, and it's time he paid for my father's death, and for standing back and doing nothing while Dempsey's idiot father slowly killed my mother."

Jolie let her hands stroke the back of Liam's head, her fingernails threading through his hair.

What he'd suffered after Renzo's take over was by and large a thousand times worse than what she had suffered. It had been so many years that sometimes she forgot Renzo gained control the way he had. The entire pack seemed to forget it at times, too, only to be harshly reminded whenever Renzo went on a rampage.

"They'll be better off with you," Jolie said. "You'll be a

better leader, and most everyone there remembers your father. They respect him. They'll probably follow you even if you don't kill Renzo."

Liam nodded. "But he'll die anyway. I saw it in his eyes. If I show my face again, he will fight me. If I don't go back, he will hunt us down. He won't be able to handle the way I left—with some of his betas, you, and his pride crushed the way it was."

"Makes sense. So you're going to challenge him before he can come looking for us?"

"Yes," Liam said, another growl, but this one sounded much more promising as his hands moved across her waist. "After I've had you."

That warmth, that energy inside Jolie's body woke right the hell up as Liam's hands slid up her shirt.

"They can't see us in the front seat?" she asked, not bothering to glance over at the tinted glass.

"I doubt it," Liam said.

Meaning he didn't know, but since Jolie couldn't hear what they were saying or doing up there, and could hardly see them, she got the feeling they were perfectly safe back here.

She pushed herself into his lap. "Feels kind of naughty to be doing this when Franky and Josh are two feet away."

The glowing lust in Liam's eyes didn't stop blazing, and the smirk the curled up at the corner of his mouth didn't stop him from looking incredibly sexy either.

"Yes, it does," he admitted.

"You're dirty. Literally and figuratively."

"I am." He pulled her shirt off her head. She lifted her arms to help with that.

He was also hard. Even with her jeans still between them, it was difficult to not notice the firm length of his cock pointing up at her.

Really, he wasn't so bloody and dusty that they couldn't do this, and it really was kind of exciting, knowing there were other people only a couple of feet away.

It wasn't difficult for Jolie to talk herself into it. She didn't need much convincing at all. That probably made her something of a *hussy*, as the elders in the pack would say. "I guess we're not going to get much private time for the next little while."

"Which means we should take advantage of our time together while we can," Liam confirmed, and this time, his growl sent a shiver up her arms. Every hair on the back of her neck stood on end, and the rush of pleasure from that noise alone was enough to make the bottom of her belly melt with warmth and heat.

She wanted him. She wanted him so bad it hurt.

"All right, alpha," Jolie said. "While we've still got the time alone together, rock my world."

THE END OF THIS STORY
NEXT: THE WILD WOLF'S WIFE VOLUME 3

CHAPTER 18

"Renzo might've said he wouldn't fight this anymore, but we can bet everything we have that Dempsey won't let this go." Liam's green eyes danced, as though anticipating the thought of a fight. "He'll disobey Renzo if he has to. He's too embarrassed to want to let this drop."

Jolie pushed some of her hair behind her ears. Her normal, human ears. The wolf ears that popped out on top of her head, as if she was a living, breathing, anime character, weren't there. Mainly because she was just barely managing to hold herself together.

The tension of the situation, and watching Liam take charge like this was definitely doing it for her.

"You really think he's going to want to challenge you again?" she asked, desperate to keep her mind off her lust. She couldn't stop looking at the way Liam's already huge arms seemed to flex whenever he reached out and pointed at a spot on the little map he and the five betas around him had made up.

It was pretty good, considering he hadn't spent more than

two minutes inside the pack since he'd been kicked out so many years prior. The five betas surrounding the table would have had a hand in that. It had just been there when Jolie woke up from her tent that morning.

The five betas, all men, most of them her age but some younger, looked at her as if she'd grown a second head.

"You know this is Dempsey we're talking about here, right?" Mitch asked. "I mean, what the hell do you think he's going to be doing?"

Mitch and Jordan were barely twenty years old. Not that Jolie and Liam were much older and wiser, but it made sense, given the way he just spoke to the mate of his new alpha.

When Liam growled at Mitch, Mitch's eyes immediately widened, and he snapped his mouth shut, shifted from foot to foot, and cleared his throat. "Sorry, Alpha."

Liam nodded, exhaling a gruff noise. "Don't let it happen again."

"We won't, Alpha," Josh said, glaring at Mitch, as if he and the rest of the betas had something to apologize for in the first place.

They used to be betas for Renzo, though they did a lot of Dempsey's dirty work, too. Now that they'd betrayed Dempsey and followed Liam, their fates were sealed. Liam was their alpha now. Liam was the man whose orders they had to follow. Liam was the wolf they'd put all their hopes into for something better.

And they all looked at Liam with a spark of hero worship in their eyes, as if they collectively had man-crushes on him.

Jolie had to admit, she liked that. She liked knowing Liam was so respected by the men he'd taken from Renzo and Dempsey. She liked that everything he'd done to survive after Renzo kicked him out of the pack for killing the alpha who had been hurting Liam's mother, who ultimately killed his mother, had put him in high regard to the men around him now.

Because Liam deserved it. He deserved to be respected. He deserved to be looked up to. He was the rightful alpha of the pack. His father had been a good and fair leader who rarely needed to use any force whenever someone became unruly.

Everyone respected him too much to let it get to that.

Renzo ruined that when he came and made the challenge, he and his alphas overtaking the pack, and in the final challenge, when he'd killed Liam's father and took over, no one forgot about it.

Then Liam's mother had been given as a mate to Renzo's friend, and Dempsey's father, essentially making them stepbrothers, though Jolie knew how much Liam didn't like to think of it like that.

It made their hatred for each other all the more poetic.

Dempsey's father had been hurting Liam's mother, so Liam, a teenage boy with just enough confidence to make a stand for himself, managed to kill the man and get his revenge. Not before he could save his mother.

Dempsey always hated Liam for that, and he'd always hated Liam for being Jolie's best friend.

Jolie just didn't understand how deeply that hatred ran until Dempsey tried to take her for his mate several years later. So she ran for it, ran into the woods, desperate to find the best friend who had been cast out so many years ago, and to make what she'd always known about them a reality.

Her best friend was and had always been her true mate. That was why he'd stayed so close to the pack even after his banishment. It was why she could never let herself move on and forget about him, and she needed him to help her. To properly make his claim on her so Dempsey couldn't.

And to get him to take control of the pack that was rightfully his.

Now, Jolie was getting her wish. This was everything she could have wanted, but at the same time, she wasn't happy. This had been the thing she had been pestering Liam for ever since she found him in the woods and mated with him behind the waterfall where he'd made his home.

Now that what she'd wanted was coming to pass, she couldn't help but be sorry for ever having pushed this on him, for constantly badgering him about taking over the pack, about leading the people who were rightfully his to lead.

He could get hurt. He could get killed.

He'd proven himself in a battle against Dempsey, but he hadn't yet fought Renzo, and there was no telling if that would be a fair fight or not.

With Dempsey, the answer seemed to be a definite no. No one believed Dempsey would make a proper challenge, or that if he did, he would fight fairly.

Jolie's guts clenched at the thought of Liam getting hurt. Permanently, or otherwise.

She couldn't even stomach the suggestion that he could be killed.

Dempsey had never killed anyone before, but he'd always made it known how much he wanted to kill Liam. Revenge for the death of his father.

Jolie's heart sank.

Right. She might as well not have bothered to think about this to begin with. It was clear what would happen when Dempsey caught sight of Liam. The guy didn't just have revenge on his mind for his father, but when Liam bloodied Dempsey's face and body, stuffed a belt in his mouth, and presented him to Renzo like a pig that had just been hunted…

Yeah, Liam was right. Dempsey wasn't going to let something like that go.

"I'll make my challenge to Renzo known tomorrow at sunset." Liam looked up at the sky, as though expecting to see what he was looking for so early in the day.

Jolie knew what he was looking for.

"The moon'll be nice and full."

The betas around the folding table nodded, eyes eager. Josh cracked his knuckles, as though he couldn't wait for a fight.

Any alpha could take over a pack, but there was something about taking it during a full moon that gave a more official feel to the whole thing. It was definitely the sort of thing that other shifters in packs liked to be aware of whenever there was an attempted take-over.

She had no idea why that was a thing. Wolves with their moons could be a little excessive sometimes, as far as she was concerned. Jolie never cared for howling at a full moon, or respecting it as much as the rest of the pack. Then again, she'd never had the undeniable instinct to howl passionately up at the moon until she'd called for Liam. Called to her mate to come for her when she'd been Renzo's prisoner.

Liam's powerful hand touched her shoulder. Even with that gentle press of his fingers, she felt the energy of him, his strength, and heat. Jolie jumped.

Liam pulled back suddenly. "Are you all right?" His brows pressed almost completely together, his gaze surveying her up and down, as though searching for an injury.

Jolie shook her head quickly, glancing around at the other betas who were also looking at her. She had to recover fast. "I'm fine. Everything's great." Even as she said it, the words came out sounding very much like a lie.

She got the feeling that everyone around the table knew it, too.

"Can I talk to you? Alone?"

Liam didn't so much as look at the five betas around the table. It was as if they weren't there. "Of course."

Jolie smiled, sighing. She couldn't help but be relieved as she went to him, pressing herself against his powerful body, tucking herself beneath his arm and letting him curl it around her shoulders. She smiled up at him, loving the way his lips pulled back in a grin as he stared down at her.

There was a time when he would not have smiled like that for anyone. Not even her. Things had changed so much since they'd found each other again.

"Not over there," she said when Liam led her towards the vehicles they'd stolen from Dempsey and Renzo.

Right. There was no standing up in the small tents they'd acquired. Really, those had been purchased mostly for Jolie's sake, since betas and alphas could handle the outdoors better than an omega could.

Liam blinked. "It will be quiet. No one will see us or hear us in the back seat."

It was still too close, besides, the betas wouldn't be able to see or hear them, but they would know what was going on inside those vehicles when they started to rock back and forth.

"Let's find somewhere else."

Maybe it was the way she looked up at him, because just then, something in his eyes seemed to click, and she could tell. He knew what she really wanted from him, even if she had no idea what the hell she was going to say to him when it ended.

"All right then, let's find somewhere private where we can talk."

"Right. *Talk.*"

It was the *private* part of that sentence Jolie was more concerned with.

CHAPTER 19

*L*iam let Jolie take the lead, which she liked.

She liked the fact that he was letting himself drag behind just enough so she was in front of him, holding tightly to his hand as she led him deeper and deeper into the woods.

She really had no idea where the hell she was going, but she did know that she wanted to get as far away from the other betas as she possibly could. Because she needed an excellent sense of hearing to know for sure if she was far enough away from them, she let her wolf ears back out. They popped through her hair on top of her head, twitching as she listened for any sound of their conversation.

When she couldn't hear it anymore, she kept going, searching for a quiet, clean place away from any badgers or other nests. Somewhere she could enjoy her mate all to herself.

"I think I would enjoy this eagerness of yours all the more if I knew it wasn't coming from your fear for me."

Jolie glared at the man she loved over her shoulder, though she didn't stop walking. "You could tell that?"

He lifted an auburn brow at her. "I could practically smell it on you. So could the others."

That put some heat in her cheeks, and not in a good way. It was almost enough to make her forget about the lust that tightened through her body, and made the hairs on the back of her neck stand up.

"Watch yourself." Liam quickly grabbed her by the shoulder, steering her away from several pine branches that pointed right out.

Jolie sucked back a hard breath, narrowly avoiding getting her eyes poked out by several spiky, long wooden fingers.

"Uh, thanks," she said, then immediately forgot about what almost happened. "Tell me you know somewhere we can go for this."

"I do. We've been gathering water not too much farther from here," Liam said. "The stream is actually connected to the waterfall where I was living. There will be fish if you're hungry."

"I'm not hungry for food." She looked back up at him, noted the dilating that happened in his eyes. His tongue darted out to wet his lips. He was bare-chested. Liam didn't make a habit of wearing many clothes, but even when he did, he was so big and lean that any t-shirt he wore stretched out nicely, leaving nothing to the imagination.

Had he been wearing something now, she would have seen the tight expanse of his perfect chest, the budding of his nipples, as well as his abs through the material.

Since he wasn't, she got a nice view of those things right in the flesh.

Sometimes she wasn't sure what she liked more. The sight of him punishing his shirts and stretching them out, especially when he got them wet, or when he was in the bare flesh.

At least with his shirt off, she could see the perfect V shape that happened around his waist and pelvis. God, he was so perfect. She hated that Liam had been forced to live the life he'd had, but she was happy it hadn't broke him.

"Yes, keep staring at me like that, Jolie," Liam said in a voice that was nearly a purr.

A purr that brought a pleasurable shiver all the way up and down her spine.

"I might not get you to that stream."

"What will you do if you can't?"

His eyes danced as he yanked her to his body so they were pressing against each other. He stared down at her as if she was something he could eat. "I would rip your clothes off right here, get your sweet breasts in my hands and mouth, and impale you on my cock. That's what you want, isn't it?"

He really didn't need to ask, though she nodded anyway.

Jolie didn't dare look down. She knew what she would see. She could make it out partly through her peripheral vision already.

The bulge forming between his legs. His cock rising to attention, entirely for her. She wanted her hands on it, her mouth on it, and she wanted it inside her.

The knowledge that her mate and alpha was going into battle was apparently bringing out the desperate little floozy in her.

"Maybe it's a good idea," she said, glancing around. Her wolf ears picked up the sounds of water not too much farther away, but she was impatient. Her clothes had never felt this tight on her body before. She was practically suffocating in them. "Stop here. Stop, this is good."

Liam didn't try to stop her. He didn't mention they were closing in on their destination and they only needed a few more steps to get to where they needed to go.

No, he pulled her into his arms instead, and when his

mouth came down onto hers, capturing her lips, kissing them, owning them, her knees trembled and heart fluttered.

Yes, this was what she'd been thinking about all damned day, and all day yesterday.

They'd made love frantically in the back of one of Renzo's stolen vehicles when they made their getaway, when Liam had stormed in like a badass conquerer, Dempsey his hostage, and taking five betas for himself, but it hadn't been nearly enough.

Jolie wanted more. She needed more.

She gasped for breath as her mouth separated from his. Her hands touched the rough hairs on his jaw and cheeks before she pushed her fingers through his now short auburn hair.

"I need you, right now. I can't take it anymore."

"You're not the only one." Liam's hands grasped her waist hard enough that she knew his fingers would leave bruises later. He yanked her hips forward. Jolie's heart did a little jolting thing when she felt the hard length of his cock through their clothes.

She smiled, feeling the need to joke around a little. "That for me?"

"No, it's for Josh."

Jolie jerked back, blinking at him, at the utterly deadpan way he just said that.

He was always so serious that, for a hair of a second, she thought he might just be serious and maybe wanted to get someone else in on this.

The slow pull of his lips into a smile had her exhaling hard, shaking her head. "Don't scare me like that!"

He scoffed. "You thought I was serious?"

"Well, you're always a little serious."

"Not anymore." Liam shook his head. "Not since you came back to me." Then his mouth was on hers again, the kiss softer, but no less commanding, and Jolie knew exactly what it meant when she felt the touch of his tongue against her lips.

He wasn't asking permission. No, he was just letting her know it was coming before he spread her lips apart with his tongue, licking her deep in her mouth. And she loved it. Jolie's head fell back, her mouth falling open just a little wider, giving her mate all the room he needed, giving all of herself over to him.

He could do whatever the fuck he wanted with her and Jolie could die a happy woman. Liam had proven again and again that he knew what he was doing when it came to her body, and his hands were not idle as he kissed her. They came up, giving her breasts a teasing squeeze, hard enough to let her know they were there before pulling back before she could get enough pleasure from the rough squeezing.

Of course, she couldn't complain when immediately after his hands really did start pulling at her clothes. Their mouths parted again as Liam yanked her shirt above her head. Even with it off, only her bra between his wicked mouth and her pert nipples, she felt as if the heat in the air around her suddenly spiked. It was warm out, but it hadn't been this damned hot.

When Liam's mouth attacked the flesh of her collarbone, searing her skin, burning her more than she thought possible whenever they happened to touch, she threw her head back and moaned.

Her tail came out. It whipped around excitedly behind her until Liam's hands slid around her waist, touching the base of the end, gripping it.

She barely managed to stop the wagging, but then it didn't matter because Liam was undoing her little belt with the heart buckle. The second it was loose, he worked the button and zipper of her jeans. The sound of those metal teeth parting made her bite her lower lip. Even when she spread her legs, they were tight enough that he had trouble getting them, and her little pink panties, down her thighs.

"Just rip them off." She was hot and bothered enough to want to watch him do that, to want to see the physical show of his strength and power before he plunged into her.

Liam raised his eyes to her, which made her suddenly notice how he was bent over her chest. "I want to, sweetheart, trust me, I do."

She growled at him. "All I'm hearing is that you're not going to do it."

"Unless you want to walk around with your bare ass showing to all the betas, it's not the best idea." Liam growled back at her. "And I happen to like that this ass is only for me to see."

He reached down, his palms grabbing, fingers digging into the flesh of her ass. Jolie gasped, her hips arching forward, even though she wanted nothing more than to push back into his hands.

Which she did the second she was able.

"This is for me. Agreed?"

Jolie nodded.

"Not for anyone else."

She got the feeling they weren't talking about the betas who were loyal to him anymore.

Fine by her. "Definitely. You're the only one."

Dempsey was nothing compared to him. He was insane to ever think she would accept a mating with him lying down. Liam was the only one that mattered. The only one who'd ever mattered.

"Just make sure you stay alive. Make sure you come back to me."

"Nothing will keep me away from you. Believe that with everything you've got because I sure as hell do."

Jolie had to lift her feet as Liam pulled her shoes off. He scratched her accidentally as he yanked off her jeans one leg at a time after that, tossing them over a nearby branch, leaving her wearing nothing but her bra and a smile.

His hands touched the back of her knees, putting just enough pressure on them that he easily pulled her down onto his lap.

She came willingly, straddling him, knowing it was exactly what he wanted her to do.

Jolie curled her arms around Liam's neck, touching the soft hairs that grew at his nape.

Liam never broke eye contact with her, and she couldn't look away from him, even as she saw his one arm moving around between them, heard the metallic grind of his button and zipper spreading apart, and then felt the heat rising between them.

"I want it inside me," she said, thrusting her pelvis forward, feeling the hard length of his shaft against her sex.

Oh God, maybe she shouldn't have done that because all of a sudden it felt as if she couldn't hold onto the orgasm building within her.

Liam didn't attempt to play coy, didn't make a show of teasing her and didn't hold her to her pain and misery for long.

His other arm looped around her waist, pulling her up and onto her knees.

She knew what to do after that. Some things didn't need words to be understood, and as she adjusted herself, she felt the soft head pressing against her opening, and at Liam's growl, she impaled herself down onto his cock, crying out from the sharp pleasure, the sensation of being filled, and then locking them together as she curled her legs around his waist.

Liam growled, clenched his eyes shut for a few seconds, and when he opened them, they were a bright shade of red.

The red of lust, of a wild animal with his mate, and it excited her like nothing else in the world could.

"That's it, sweetheart," he said through clenched teeth. "Now *move*."

CHAPTER 20

She moved all right. Jolie moved her hips, turned and thrust, up and down, circular, with wild abandon, because as much as she didn't want to say it and didn't want to admit it, she made love to him as if it was the last time they would ever do it.

She also made love to him hoping it wasn't the last time, but she couldn't help herself.

She touched him everywhere. Her hands wouldn't hold still. Jolie tried holding onto the back of his neck for purchase, but it wasn't enough. She had to touch his tight nipples; she played with them, eager to draw a reaction from him, any kind of reaction.

She did. He growled at her. The best kinds of growls as he pumped his cock back and forth inside her, again and again, so Jolie kept doing it. She kept touching him.

When she was too afraid that it was getting old, she kissed him, on his jaw, and then his neck, sucking on the spot where his pulse raced. She bit that spot, too, desperate to leave her mark, to bruise him, to give him something nice to remember her by when he went off to fight.

She wanted him to remember what they were fighting for when he was right in the thick of things. She didn't want him to forget for a single second how much she loved him.

The orgasm within her wouldn't be contained. Not with the way Liam moved inside her, his cock stretching her inner walls to the max and driving her wild. That warmth, that ball of pressure, just kept getting bigger and bigger until there was nothing left for her to hold it back with.

As hard as she tried, it wasn't enough, and Jolie threw her head back, crying out as it finally hit her and hit her hard.

She grasped tightly to the back of Liam's neck, and then it wasn't enough as she dug her small claws into his back. Liam growled, a low, dangerous note in her ear as she felt the warmth of him spilling inside her as the push and pull of his hips became a harder, almost violent thing.

His body was still warm, that was the one thing Jolie noticed when he finished. He was still warm, and the sound of their combined breathing, harsh as it was, was loud in the air.

And Jolie was happy. Happier than she thought she had the right to be, considering what was going to happen tomorrow when the sun went down and the full moon came out.

Jolie sighed, soaking in the heat of Liam's body, letting the pleasure of what they'd just done really wash over her. She kissed the spot on his throat where a tiny red mark was forming, and, hopefully, later on a little bruise.

Which was about when she noticed the bloody mess she'd made of his back.

"Jesus, Liam! Look what I did to you."

"It's fine," he said, his voice that tone of growly that usually happened whenever he was pleased and lulled by something. Usually an orgasm. "Your claws are small, they couldn't have done that much damage."

"Uh, it's pretty bloody," she said, unable to look away from her work.

Yeah, her claws were small, but holy crap, she should have noticed when she'd scratched him like that. It would have hurt to high hell and back if he'd scratched her up like that.

"Will it heal quickly? Fast enough for your fight tomorrow?"

"If it doesn't then I know the perfect woman to bandage it for me so I don't go stinking of blood and giving away our position."

Jolie's heart warmed at that. The warmth actually spread throughout her chest and to the rest of her body. Down her arms and legs, up her neck, and into her cheeks and ears. She could spend an entire winter naked and in the woods with Liam, and Jolie was positive she'd be comfortable the entire time with just the things he said to her.

"Well, maybe we should get this cleaned up in the stream before heading—"

A soft rustle in the trees caught her attention, made her ears flick towards the noise.

Liam must have heard it as well because he immediately turned his gaze in the same direction.

Jolie didn't see it at first, but when she did, she shrieked.

Liam yanked himself out of her arms and flew at the pair of eyes that had been watching them through the leaves and branches in the shrubs and trees while Jolie scrambled to cover herself.

Her heart pounded, and not in the good way it had been doing just a couple of minutes ago as she stuffed one leg, and then the other, back into her jeans.

Someone had been watching her and Liam. The entire time? Fuck, she didn't know, she'd been distracted.

Dammit! She hadn't put on her panties. They were her only pair and she basically had to wash and dry them every other day to feel even close to being clean, and she didn't want whoever that pervert had been to get at them. She shoved them into her pocket, hoping no one would see the bright pink until she managed to sneak them back on at a later point in time.

Next came her shoes, and she ran back to camp, calling for anyone who could get to her and help her right now.

All five of them came for her, meeting her after what seemed like an eternity of shouting, but could have only been a couple of minutes.

"What's going on?" Josh demanded, eyeing her up and down. She just knew he and the others could smell the sex on her. "What happened?"

Jolie pointed back the way she came. "Someone was watching me and Liam! He went off and chased whoever it was."

She didn't get the chance to finish that sentence before four of the five betas took off chasing after the pervert in question, following their alpha all the way to the end.

It left her alone with Mitch, who noticeably didn't put his hands on her. "Let's go back. The alpha will want you kept safe."

Jolie looked at him, at the worry in his eyes. She got along with Mitch well enough when they had been under Renzo's rule, but she could never remember him looking at her quite like that before.

As much as she wished she hadn't run away like a complete coward, fighting with him, wanting to go back and see what happened would just get in everyone's way.

That was dangerous at this point. She couldn't have that.

Jolie nodded, allowing Mitch to walk with her back to the camp.

Mitch sighed when they got back, glancing around.

"What is it?" Jolie asked.

"Nothing's changed."

Jolie didn't understand at first, but then she did.

Right, that could have been a trap set out to get her and the others out of the way so someone could ruin their setup. The tires on the vehicles could have been slashed, their tents destroyed, supplies ruined, anything.

She hadn't even thought to be worried about that.

Now that she was thinking about it, and knew everything was all right, she went back to focusing on Liam.

"Did you see who was out there watching you?"

"No, I didn't hear or smell anything either."

Mitch looked at her funny. "How close could he have gotten to you?"

Her cheeks immediately burned. She couldn't look him in the face to answer that question. "We were a little distracted."

It seemed to take Mitch a minute before he understood, and when he did, his neck and ears brightened. "Oh. Right."

Jolie wished she hadn't bothered to look at him. It was too humiliating.

Thankfully, it didn't take long before Liam and the others returned, with an extra person with them.

Jolie's eyes flew wide. "*Red?*"

Liam had him by the back of the neck. He was still naked from their lovemaking, though sweaty and dirty now from his run in the woods.

And he didn't look remotely happy as he shoved Red forward, a hard glare for the man as Red stumbled and barely managed to stop himself from falling to his knees.

Red's clothes were dirty, as if he'd been on the move for a while. His red hair was all over the place and he had a fresh scratch down the side of his cheek. That, along with what appeared to be some dark mud on the front of his clothes, suggested he'd been tackled.

Jolie didn't have to ask to know who did that.

She glanced at her mate. Liam wouldn't stop staring hot lasers at Red.

Red dusted himself off, clearing his throat as he briefly looked up at her, and then back at Liam. "I'm sorry, okay? It was an accident."

"It better damn well have been!" Liam roared. His fangs popped right out of his mouth. A vein pulsed heavily along the side of his neck, and it honestly looked as if Red was the luckiest guy in the world for not having both of his arms and legs broken.

Jolie still couldn't get over the fact that he was here. The heat of her humiliation was still fresh with her, but she suddenly couldn't stop smiling over the fact that he was standing right there. He'd come to join them.

She went to him and wrapped her arms around him as tight as she could. "You came," she sighed. "I can't believe you're here."

Red barely touched her. "Yeah, me neither."

He didn't sound so happy. Jolie pulled back quickly. "Is everything okay? What about your family? Are they all right?"

Red pressed his lips together. He barely looked at her. It was clear this was the last place in the world he wanted to be, and Jolie's heart sank just a little.

"They're fine, for now. I have to be quick about this. I snuck away. I know what you're going to do tomorrow when the moon is full, and so does Renzo. He's waiting for you to attack."

Jolie gripped his hands. "You risked everything to come here and tell us that."

It wasn't a question. She knew that's what he'd done, and she couldn't have been more grateful to him in that moment.

"I could have said as much," Liam growled, stepping over to them.

He only needed to glance down at Jolie's hands holding onto Red's before Red cleared his throat and immediately pulled back.

"Red's our friend," Jolie said. "You don't have to be jealous of him."

Liam said nothing and he turned back to Red. "Are you going to help us with the fight?"

Red nodded. "Much as I can, I will. I'll lend my strength, but again, they have to know I'm gone by now. I made sure to send my mom and sister out to get groceries an hour or so after I left to go hunting. They wouldn't have gone back, but there's no telling what could have happened after I left."

"Smart," Franky said, his arms crossed. "Smarter than when we all left."

"Is everyone else okay?" Josh asked.

A thin knife of guilt got Jolie right in the chest, through her ribs, and into her heart. She'd been so wrapped up in her own happiness with Liam, with her own worries and fears for the man, that she'd completely stopped thinking about all the things the betas left behind when they changed their loyalties to him. They had families of their own, friends, and ties that would normally bind people to a pack even if they weren't altogether happy with the alpha.

Renzo could have taken his frustration out on them after they left. Jolie didn't want to think that Renzo was that sort of alpha. Aside from killing Liam's father in the fight for the pack all those years ago, he'd only ever been just a little on the strict side.

"They're fine," Red said, putting everyone out of their misery. "Renzo didn't punish them. He was angry, and Dempsey threw his weight around a little and made some threats, but Renzo is keeping him under control."

"Dempsey didn't hurt anyone, did he?"

Red shook his head. "No."

It was the way he briefly glanced away from her when he answered, before looking her right in the eyes, that made Jolie believe something was not quite right. As if he was trying to hide the fact that he couldn't look her in the eyes when he said the word *no*.

Okay, interesting. That didn't hint towards good things.

"So he knows we're coming, we figured as much," Liam said, his massive arms and chest appearing that much broader and stronger when he crossed his arms. "I just need enough of a distraction to get to him and properly challenge him."

Jolie looked at her mate, really looked at him. She tried to find any indication at all that he'd caught that same hint of something wrong, but he gave no outward signs that he noticed anything. He *did* notice it, though. Jolie could tell that much. She and Liam hadn't been properly mated for long, and the time they'd spent apart from each other, growing up without each other, may have meant there were still some gaps to fill, but she *knew* him. Liam thought something was off as much as Jolie did. He was just better at keeping that to himself.

"Look, there's something you should know, and I don't think you'll have seen this one coming," Red said, and this time, he made sure to look at everyone as he spoke.

It was the tone of his voice that made Jolie lean in just a little closer. What had his eyes looking so wild and frantic?

Red seemed to have everyone's attention, and the betas didn't dare blink as they looked at him.

Liam seemed to be the only one who hadn't flinched, who barely reacted to the tense aura surrounding Red. "Out with it."

Red wet his lips, nodding. "Renzo isn't the alpha anymore. He handed over control to Dempsey right after you left."

CHAPTER 21

Jolie didn't get it at first. She needed some clarification because for a split second it kind of sounded as if Red just suggested Renzo was no longer an alpha.

When she asked, Red shook his head. "I mean, no, he's still an alpha, but he's just not *the* alpha. He's not in charge anymore. He handed it over to Dempsey. Dempsey's calling all the shots, he's making all the calls, and he's still mad about what happened."

Red's gaze finally locked onto Jolie's, and Jolie didn't like the pity she saw within his eyes.

"He's really, *really* pissed off. I don't know if he still wants you for a mate, but he's been talking about you. He wants to hurt you at the very least." Red looked to Liam. "Both of you."

"No one is touching her."

Jolie turned to her mate. She could swear that she saw long, coarse hairs sprouting out through the pores of Liam's skin. His eyes blazed with fire. If she looked close enough, she was sure she might actually see a physical flame behind his irises.

Jolie shivered. The strength of his inner alpha was coming out. She didn't often see the massive wolf he'd become, but she sensed it. It was right there, growling low and deep beneath the surface of Liam's human skin, the only barrier that kept the animal from popping out and destroying absolutely everything around it.

A piece of her, the omega side, wanted to run. Or present her belly.

The other side of her, the side that was Liam's loyal mate, wanted to tear both of their clothes off to have one more go with the powerful creature before her.

Because Liam was powerful. He was powerful and he was hers. He would protect her, just as he'd promised.

"I never said that," Red said quickly.

Liam hardly seemed to hear Red. "If that little bitch Dempsey thinks he can somehow get through me, I'd like to see him try. He could never catch me when I was constantly outrunning him, he could never beat me in a fight, and when push came to shove, I made him eat dirt, and I'll make him eat it again." Liam turned to the betas around him, the men who had seen first hand the battle he was talking about, the one Jolie had missed because she'd been too busy playing damsel in distress in Renzo's house.

They stared at Liam as if he was their own personal hero, their favorite movie star, a Navy Seal, and even Batman all rolled into one.

He had their full attention.

"That is our pack!" Liam roared, more fur sprouting, more of that powerful animal coming to the surface.

The guys around him, with the exception of Red, all cheered.

"Dempsey is not fit to lead you, anyone else, or even a dog!"

Another hard cheer. The air surrounding them was too

good, too excited, and Jolie couldn't help the way it affected her.

Her blood sizzled.

"We'll walk right in there and take back what belongs to us! Anyone who wants to stay loyal to those failures will be cast out with them!"

Again, the men cheered.

Jolie didn't know much about inspirational speeches, and she was pretty sure that was not one of them, not really. It seemed more as if Liam was playing to their desire for a victory, that he was playing to their confidence and their belief in him.

If that was the case, he nailed that part perfectly. She felt almost as if she could follow her mate onto the battle field with the strength of a beta, or even an alpha, in her blood.

Then Liam looked at her, their eyes locking together, and once again, she struggled against the urge to leap into his arms, to kiss him in front of the betas around her, and to make love to him. Crazy as that sounded, a piece of her wanted to show off to these betas that, as deep as their loyalties went, and despite the man-crushes they all had on him, Liam was hers.

He was hers and he belonged to no one else. She would always have that over the betas around her, even if she didn't have their strength or their ability to rush into a battle with Liam, to keep him safe.

He didn't need anyone to keep him safe. He was powerful enough to take on Renzo and Dempsey. He was powerful enough to stay one step ahead of the both of them even as a teenager.

Jolie had been worried in the beginning, but now her confidence was more than boosted. Maybe with Liam's leadership and strength combined, a small pack of this size would be enough to take back their home. Especially if a few other betas they'd left behind decided to fight for Dempsey. They might have this in the bag.

"Wait, wait a minute," Mitch said, the first to come off the high from Liam's war cries. It seemed he was going to be the killjoy when it came down to it. "I don't get it. It has to mean something that Renzo would just let Dempsey take over. Liam kicked Dempsey's ass the last time. Why just give him command of the pack?"

"Because he knows he'll lose and he doesn't want to get the living piss beat out of him," Franky said, lips pulled back in the biggest grin Jolie had ever seen on his face.

She thought about it. Mitch was right, something was off, but it also did kind of make sense for Renzo to not want to be the one to face the actual challenge.

"Maybe," she started, thinking as she went along. "It really could just be strategic. Dempsey is younger than he is, and still strong, despite what happened. Also, there's the matter of Liam's parents." Jolie looked at her mate, not glancing away at the flicker of pain that appeared, and then disappeared, from Liam's eyes. "I don't like bringing it up, but maybe Renzo is worried Liam will kill him in the battle for the pack? A way to get back at him for what happened to his father?" Jolie wet her lips, looking back at Liam. "I'm sorry." She had to say it. It felt almost wrong to bring up what happened to Liam's father in that fight so long ago. It was the reason why they almost hadn't mated with each other, even after Liam saved her from Dempsey that first time.

He'd been angry, and she understood why.

They'd always kind of known about this thing between them, even back when they were too young to understand the concept of what it meant to really be someone's mate.

Jolie didn't like thinking about it. It was her one regret—that she hadn't gone with him when she should have.

"Renzo handing over control of the pack won't stop me from killing him," Liam growled.

That seemed to put a quick stop to the good mood of the betas around him. They all looked at Liam as if they thought he was slightly off his rocker.

"Killing another alpha like that is murder," Josh said carefully. "If he's not the alpha you're challenging for the pack, and he's not attacking you, then it's not legal. You can't even claim self-defense for that."

Liam growled again. The way he clenched his fists wasn't lost on Jolie either. She went to him, reaching out, sliding her fingers down the tight flesh of his forearm, her hand slipping into his. She was glad when he didn't yank himself away, but his body didn't relax for her either. He was still wound up. He was angry and glaring at all the men around him. It was as if they were all kids again and someone had broken his favorite toy.

The difference was they were no longer children. They weren't young teenagers either, and like Jolie, these guys were going to have to get used to the fact that taking care of himself for so long out in the wild had changed the person they had once called a friend.

It was going to take more than just pointing out the obvious to Liam, that killing Renzo if he wasn't the alpha challenger was an act of murder, to convince him it wasn't the sort of thing he wanted to be doing.

"Liam." Jolie reached up, touched his cheek, and turned his attention down to her. "Whether you kill Dempsey or not, I'll still be here for you. I know it's not what you want to hear, but if Renzo isn't the challenger, then for me, please don't kill him."

The way Liam's throat vibrated as he growled was a reminder of the strength he barely managed to contain. The wolf was right behind those eyes, and it was as wild and angry as Liam was.

"What do you suggest I do with him when I get my hands on him? Banish him?" Liam snorted. "Like that would make up for what he did to me, my father, my mother."

Jolie swallowed hard, nodding. She couldn't help the burn that started up in her eyes either. She'd loved his parents, too. They had been kind to her, and now she had to convince Liam, for the sake of his own soul, and the respect of the pack, to not avenge them.

"Well, banishment probably isn't even close to being good enough if you wanted to make him understand what he did to you and your parents, but," she added, hoping this next part would help out at least a little. "No one said you had to take it easy on him either. An alpha wolf can still survive banishment with a broken arm or two."

Liam blinked widely down at her. He even jerked back a little.

Jolie softly smiled up at him. "Was that a little mean?"

"Holy shit," Red said, his mouth gaping. "That might've been the meanest thing I ever heard you say."

Jolie shrugged. "Well, I need to help my alpha get some satisfaction out of this. If Renzo wants to play the game like that then he's going to walk away with a permanent limp."

A nervous chuckle worked through the guys around her. Franky nudged Jordan in the ribs. "Walk away with a limp," he said with a chuckle.

"Limp away," Jordan corrected.

Even Liam started to smile, the anger in his eyes leaving, but that wild animal was still present, and also smiling down at her. "And here I thought you were supposed to tame my wild beast."

Suddenly brave, Jolie pressed her palms to Liam's chest,

batting her eyes up at him. "I'll do that for you when we're in bed. This is for your own peace of mind."

The betas around her groaned collectively, then some laughed.

Liam never took his gaze away from her. The heated fire of lust returned, and his smile showed off the whites of his teeth. Jolie didn't look away from him, and she felt the heat of his palm snaking around her waist, pulling her closer to his hard body.

Which also worked nicely to hide his naked cock.

"Uh, are you two going to need some time alone before we pack up, alpha?"

Liam suddenly pulled Jolie closer, lifting her into his arms, apparently not caring who saw his erection.

Alphas.

"Give me an hour. We'll be done by then," Liam said.

Jolie laughed as her mate carried her off as if she was his prize.

CHAPTER 22

It took them a little more than an hour, and by then Liam had managed to bring Jolie to those monumental heights again and again to the point where she didn't have the energy to be embarrassed by what happened, and even when they finally made it back to camp and everything was already packed up and put away, the betas looking at both her and Liam expectantly, she just smiled at them and shrugged.

Her alpha wanted her, and she wasn't in the mood to deny him. Really, it was instinct, so it wasn't as if anyone could hold it against her.

She didn't think they did. The smiles she got were good-natured and fun. Jolie half expected someone to give her a quick thumb's up, but it didn't happen. She hadn't felt this close to anyone in her pack since, well, since after Liam had been banished. Whether it was the fact that she was in a smaller group that made the difference, or her general good mood after flying high on pleasure for so long, she didn't know, and Jolie decided she didn't much care either.

Liam managed to get a pair of pants on when he hopped

back into the back seat of one of the black vehicles with her. Jolie snuggled up to his side as Josh and Red hopped up front.

Josh took the driver's seat. It seemed no one quite trusted Red to do the driving just yet.

Jolie grinned up at her mate. She could almost forget about what they would be doing in just over twenty-four hours. "You know, you're going to have to start making a better habit of wearing clothes more often, right?"

Liam glanced down at her, and then back up, as if he was watching the two people in the front seat. "Shifters are used to nudity."

"True." Jolie circled her finger around Liam's tight stomach, tracing all the way down to the perfect V shape that pointed below the jeans he'd put on. "But I think I'd rather have your body to myself. And, you know, we wouldn't want to risk that a human would show up and see you prancing around in your birthday suit, as nice as it is."

That got a smile out of him. It was a soft smile, but still there, and Jolie took that as a small victory.

Red cleared his throat from the front seat. "Am I allowed to know where we're going? Or is that classified?"

Jolie's brows lifted. "No one told you?"

She caught sight of Red's eyes in the rearview mirror, but he quickly looked away. "No."

Jolie glanced up at Liam, not sure if she should say anything if he'd made the decision not to.

But she did want to trust Red. He'd taken this huge risk, after all.

"Is it okay to tell him? I mean, it's not like we're going anywhere specific."

The smile melted away from Liam's lips, which was a shame because he looked so good with it on. "At this point we're just driving," Liam said. "We're holding onto what little funds we have for now, and keeping to the road will keep our scents, mostly, off the radar until it comes time to make the challenge known."

"And, will it be a full-on attack?" Red asked, looking back into the rearview mirror. "Is everyone getting in on it? Or is it going to be just you and Dempsey?"

"That's entirely dependent on him," Liam said, glancing out the passenger window. "Knowing that piece of shit, I doubt he'll want a clean match, and I'm betting the reason you ran for it was because you didn't want to be called on to fight for his side when you knew I was coming."

Red ducked his head, his face becoming almost brighter than his hair.

Jolie blinked. "I didn't think of that," she said softly.

The fact that Red left, not just because he couldn't bring himself to follow Renzo, or Dempsey in this case, but also because he didn't want Dempsey to command him to fight against his friends, or Liam, was something else entirely.

Warmth filled Jolie's chest for him, for the risk he'd taken. She knew alphas didn't like it when their mates touched other males, and Liam was no exception as a man who'd spent the last of his childhood in the wild, but she had to reach out and touch Red's shoulder. She squeezed it, ignoring the small jump.

"Thank you, Red. I knew you were going to come around for us."

Red hesitated, then nodded.

Jolie pulled back, not wanting to push her luck when it came to Liam. "Are you worried about your mother and sister?"

Red nodded. "Yeah, a lot."

Jolie often wished she could fight, wished she'd at least been born a beta, but it was at times like these when she was glad she was an omega. It meant she was better with words, and she could help to cheer Red up when he was having a hard time like this.

The other betas had pointed out how much they all appreciated it when Jolie gave them their pep talks whenever they became worried about the people they loved that they had left behind, so if this was the skill she had, she was going to use it when it was needed.

"I know that wherever they're hiding, you're mother is very proud of you, and when this is all over, you'll be able to call them back, and Liam will be in charge. Everything will be all right and you'll see them again in no time." That came out a little less elegantly than she'd thought in her mind, and the answering smile she got looked a little more forced than anything.

Jolie cleared her throat. "Are you able to call them? Let them know you made contact and that things are going fine?"

"I have a number I can call," Red said.

"You have a cell phone with you?" Liam didn't sound pleased by that. Jolie didn't understand why?

"No, I forgot to bring it. I'll have to use a gas station phone, or wherever we go to stop."

"Is that true? He didn't have a phone?" Liam asked.

Josh nodded. "Yeah, we checked when you were gone. We weren't going to forget."

Jolie tensed in her seat. "You told the betas to check Red when we were...never mind. When did you have time to do that?"

"It wasn't when Red was here," Liam said. "But I laid down some ground rules for the boys shortly after they became loyal to me. Anyone else who shows up out of the blue like Red just did gets a full pat down, after I finish with him." Liam's eyes got that spark in them again as he stared at the back of Red's head. Red seemed to know better than to turn around and face that stare.

It reminded Jolie that Liam, and the other four betas, had their hands on Red before Jolie saw them again. Liam could have given Red a proper search before bringing him back to camp, leaving the others to check again and ask a whole slew of questions while Jolie had been busy losing herself to the pleasure Liam had been giving her.

Her entire body felt like it was on fire in that moment. She wanted to sink into a deep dark hole and die.

God. That was so humiliating.

"What's the matter?" Liam asked. He took her wrist and lowered her hand, which had been hiding her face. "Why are you so red all of a sudden?"

He knew *exactly* why she was blushing like this. She could tell from the tone in his voice, and Jolie glared at him. "Why is it that every time you distract me with sex, something important is happening that I don't end up thinking of, or knowing about, until after the fact?"

Liam grinned wickedly at her. "That's possibly because I'm so good at pleasuring you?"

The heat intensified. There was an inferno in the back seat and she was going to spontaneously combust if he didn't stop. "For real, I don't think I can handle it if you keep saying that while there are other people around."

"I'm not listening to a single thing," Josh promised.

"Me neither," Red replied.

Both betas sounded as if they were in some sort of mild pain.

Which meant they had definitely been listening.

Jolie frantically searched the dashboard in the back. "Okay, where is it? That's enough?"

"Where's what?" Liam asked.

"The button that will raise the glass and separate us from them. I don't want them listening to anymore of what you say to me."

"Are you sure you don't want to be alone with me again?" Liam asked, still smiling that damned smile.

It was definitely not cute anymore. She didn't think it was sexy or cute. She thought it was annoying and she was going to end up punching something if she didn't find that damned button.

It didn't help in the least when the two men up front started laughing at the joke Liam made, and continued to laugh even when Jolie found the switch for the tinted window and held it, causing the window to rise, separating her from the riffraff up front.

It didn't stop Liam from laughing at her expense as well, dragging her close to his body once more when there was no one there to see them.

CHAPTER 23

The cars eventually came to a stop. Even though Jolie could shift into a wolf and use the bushes if she absolutely had to, she didn't like doing it at the best of times. She needed a ladies room so she could clean herself up a little, and a sandwich at the least.

Luckily, the vehicles they'd stolen needed gas. Since Renzo wasn't likely to report them stolen, all things considered, that made it safe to make a pit stop. It took some convincing before she managed to get Liam to stay outside the bathroom.

"You can't come in here with me!"

"Why not?" Liam looked at the sign with the stick figure woman on it. "Is there a camera in there that will sound an alarm if I go in?"

Jolie wanted to laugh. "No, don't be an idiot. You know there's no camera, but any other woman in there will make a noise louder than any alarm if you go in with me."

"Then we'll just say I'm in there as your service dog."

The way he purred those words, and how his hands touched her waist, was enough to make her laugh.

"*Service* dog, huh?"

Liam nodded. "Mmhmm."

She had a pretty good idea of how he wanted to service her, but there was no way he was going to be in his canine shape when he did it.

His lips against her ear tickled. Jolie squirmed out of his arms as she laughed. "God, what's gotten into you? You're so frisky lately."

His hands flew from her body as if he'd just touched an open flame, his mouth gaping and eyes horrified and wide. "*Frisky?*"

Jolie laughed again, ducking into the ladies room before he could stop her.

"I am not frisky!" he called through the door. "That is not a word used to describe me!"

"It is now!" she shot back.

Now that she finally found something that embarrassed him, she was going to have to use it.

Jolie took care of the basics, and then spent a couple of minutes in front of the mirror. She had no makeup with her. Not even a foundation or lip gloss. She suddenly became very aware of how she'd been going without those things for days. Pretty much since she'd first found Liam in the woods.

That seemed like months ago. They'd barely had the chance to enjoy each other since she'd finally worked up the courage to go after him.

Soon. Soon they would be together again, and then they could be a properly mated couple, and Liam could rebuild the life that had been taken from him.

That was going to be…so great. Jolie's heart warmed just thinking about it, and it made her want to do something with herself other than fluff her hair. If she was at a drugstore, she'd probably go through all the testers to at least put some color on her cheeks and mascara in her lashes.

Instead, she decided to go about it the old-fashioned way. When the other ladies vacated the bathroom, leaving her all to her lonesome, Jolie felt comfortable enough to start pinching her cheeks and biting her lips, desperate to at least look a little less…pale.

Somehow, spending all that time out in the sun hadn't managed to brighten her up too much. She couldn't even be called a good kind of pale. She was pasty. As in, just spent a week in a hospital, nearly dead kind of pasty. She hated that.

The added color to her face helped, and she wasn't forcing herself to smile into the mirror whenever she thought of Liam, so that brought out her eyes a little. She pushed up against her eyelashes with the sides of her fingers, trying to curl them a little.

And just for added effect, she wet her hands and sloshed a little water in her hair, dampening the strands and making the brunette color stand out as just a little darker.

She looked at herself.

Not bad, but it was as good as it was going to get without any professional products on hand. At least her ears and tail weren't out. She'd been having trouble keeping them away ever since finding Liam again.

Still, it wasn't the worst it could be. If she didn't turn the heads of at least one of the betas, she'd be disappointed.

Humming to herself, Jolie left the bathroom.

Liam was still there, leaning against the wall to the right of the door. He immediately looked down at her when she appeared, his eyes flashing, the corner of his lips twitching.

Jolie looked at him, pretending as if she hadn't just been preening and primping herself a minute ago, and totally pleased he was pretending not to notice. "Were you really waiting here this entire time?"

"I wasn't scaring the locals," he said, and this time he couldn't seem to hold back his grin.

Jolie shook her head at him. She kind of figured that a big guy like him, hanging out right beside the ladies room, would have worried someone. In fact, from the corner of her eye, Jolie could see a few women looking over at them. An air of relief surrounded them, and they went back to their own lives when it became clear the big scary man was with a woman.

"Are we almost done?"

"Almost," Liam said. "Josh took Red to make that phone call. Peter and Jordan are filling up the cars, and you're hungry, right?"

"Right." Jolie's stomach growled.

"Are you sure I can't just grab a rabbit for you?"

Jolie looked up at her mate, smiling as she linked their fingers together and walked to the door where the gas station attendant was. "Much as I love it when you hunt for me, I think if I eat Thumper one more time, I'll turn into a rabbit."

"Hmm," Liam said thoughtfully, looking her up and down as Jolie walked over to the sandwich rack.

She knew that look. "What?"

"I don't think I'd mind seeing you in a rabbit suit. Little fluffy tail and big ears on top of your head."

Jolie laughed, smacking Liam's arm, and then went back to her choices. She grabbed the chicken salad, and for later tonight, a turkey club. She was also in the mood for a lemon soda slush. The biggest one she could get.

Liam didn't appear to want anything, but just in case, she grabbed sandwiches and drinks for him and the betas as well.

It basically took up the last of the money she had.

Eek. Maybe she should have let Liam hunt for her.

Well, it didn't matter because after tomorrow night, they would be safely back home, Liam would be the alpha, and in command of the finances of the pack. They wouldn't have to worry about keeping fed after that.

Liam insisted on carrying the bags for her. Jolie didn't want to hand him everything, but at the same time, she liked that he was being all alpha and kept trying to do these things for her. In the end, she gave him two of the three bags and carried the last one herself back outside to the vehicles. They were parked along the side of the gas station now, waiting for the both of them to get back.

"I hope you guys are hungry," Jolie said, lifting her bag.

"The drinks for us, too?" Peter asked.

Liam pushed one of the bags into his hands. "There's Gatorade in the bag, fool."

The betas started to snicker. Jolie didn't understand what was so funny, though it did seem as if they were teasing Liam about something.

Were they teasing him about her? The idea stunned her. She never got the impression they were like that. Mainly because she'd never seen that kind of teasing directed at Renzo. Not because Renzo didn't have a mate, but just because of Renzo's personality. He hadn't been the type who was welcoming to that sort of play. He wanted his betas to be serious around him. Had he forced the betas to wear suits, it could have almost been a professional air he demanded of them.

Whenever the guys here teased Liam, aside from a few growls, Liam didn't do anything to retaliate. A few of those harsh growls would have been enough to convince Jolie that she didn't want to be messing with Liam either, but maybe there was something she was missing. Something that suggested to the betas it was all right, and to keep going.

Jolie liked that. She liked that Liam was making friends with his betas, and that they in turn were comfortable enough to show this side of themselves to him. It made this feel more than a pack that had been slapped together last minute. It made it feel as if they had a real bond.

"Where're Josh and Red?" Jolie asked, noticing they weren't there.

"Still making that phone call to Red's mom," Jordan said. He was the youngest of the betas at nineteen, and he pulled out a chocolate bar along with a cold breakfast burrito. He didn't look at her as he tore open the chocolate bar first, taking a huge bite off the top and closing his eyes as if it was the best thing he'd ever had. Jordan always had something of a sweet tooth.

"Josh had to go with Red to make a phone call?" Jolie looked up at Liam. "Isn't that a little excessive?"

"No," Liam said simply.

The other betas around him nodded or shrugged.

"Pretty much," Jordan replied, a mouthful of chocolate.

"For the safety of our pack," Peter agreed.

Everyone seemed to agree.

Jolie's brows lifted. "Well, okay, I guess. So long as everyone's all right with it."

"It's to keep you safe, too," Liam said, his voice much softer, his arm circling around her shoulders.

That protective feeling of alpha dominance came back when he looked down at her.

Jolie bathed in the light of that feeling. She loved it so much, though it only seemed to hit her this hard after Liam and the other betas rescued her from Renzo. She didn't like the idea that Liam might be harboring some guilty feelings over that, and that he might also be overcompensating his affection for her out of some paranoid fear that he'd nearly lost her, but she still enjoyed the attention.

The next time they were alone together, she was going to have to sit her mate down and make sure he didn't feel guilty about that anymore.

Everyone pulled out their sandwiches and started unwrapping them when Josh and Red finally came back.

Jolie sighed in relief at the sight of them. She hadn't realized she'd been holding her breath until they appeared. "There they are," she said, though everyone's attention was already on the two betas.

"Long phone call," Liam said when the two stood before him.

Red shrugged. "Had to make sure my sister was doing all right."

Liam looked at Josh, who nodded.

Jolie frowned. She didn't like that. She understood that Liam was worried and he was trying to protect her, but knowing that he was getting Josh to spy on Red irked her.

She pushed it down, digging into the bag and pulling out a fruit punch flavored Gatorade. "Red, this is for you."

He took the bottle and smiled softly down at it. "Because it's red?"

"That's your color. Are you hungry?"

"Uh, I guess I could eat. We're not going to stick around here, though, are we?"

"Why? In a hurry to be somewhere else?"

The tension in Liam's voice was impossible to ignore. Did he know something she didn't or was he having more trouble with the idea of Red being here than she'd thought?

"No," Josh said. "But I don't think it's a good idea to be holding still for very long."

"Uh oh," Peter said, hopping up to sit on the hood of the SUV. "You planning on meeting your girlfriend here?"

"No," Red muttered.

Liam looked to Josh. "Anything I need to know about that phone call?"

"His mom and sister were on the other end of the line. He

didn't tell them if he'd found us or not, but she sounded nervous enough."

"That makes sense, if she's on the run," Jolie said quickly.

She wanted to trust in Red, to believe he was here for only good reasons, but the way the betas around her were acting, as if they had picked up on something she hadn't, was enough to make her nervous.

She couldn't take it anymore. "Liam, what are you not telling me?"

Liam hardly took his steely-eyed gaze off of Red. Red stood frozen, as though waiting for the hammer to drop.

"I don't know, I've just had a bad feeling since Red got here, and you've been acting all squirrely from the first minute."

That last part was clearly directed at Red, who swallowed hard, and once again looked as if he was having trouble holding eye contact.

It was that one small thing, that inability to look them in the eyes and keep that contact, that made Jolie's heart sink. She wanted to defend him so much, but he was oozing guilt.

"Red?"

Red sucked back several deep breaths. Jolie heard the sound of his frantically beating heart, and he suddenly looked ready to bolt.

"It's not...I couldn't just..."

"Holy shit, no way," Franky said, lowering his Gatorade bottle from his mouth.

Peter looked equally stunned, as if he was about to drop his burrito. "Are you serious?"

Liam growled. "Spill it. Everything."

Red briefly bit his lips together, shaking his head, still not making eye contact. He clenched his fists, but the trembling in his body didn't give Jolie the impression he was about to shift and attack.

Not that it stopped Liam from stepping in front of her, as if he thought she needed the protection. "Red, start talking now, or I don't care who the hell sees us, I'll rip your damned throat out and eat it in front of you."

Jolie tensed. "Liam, don't, please." She quickly set her drink aside and put her hands on her mate's arms, needing to calm him down, but he didn't look as if he was aware she even touched him.

His eyes were like fire on Red.

"They saw it, they saw the way I...I wanted to follow you, I did." Red finally looked Liam in the eyes. "But they saw that. They couldn't just let it go. I *had* to."

"You piece of shit!" Liam's hand snapped out. He grabbed tightly to Red's collar, yanking him close, until they were nose to nose.

The betas suddenly stood straight. Peter slid from the hood of the SUV to back up his alpha. Jolie just wanted everything to go back to being calm and rational again.

"Okay, guys, we need to calm down. There are people around and cameras are watching us. *Liam*," Jolie tried not to beg, she really did, but that was just the way her voice came out sounding. "*Please*, put him down. He's still your friend. We can deal with this later."

"He's no friend of mine," Liam grumbled, that same dangerous growl rippling through his chest and throat. He shoved Red back. Red stumbled, but he stayed on his feet.

"I didn't want to do this!" he insisted desperately.

"He could be telling the truth," Jolie said, her mind racing to think of anything that would make what he'd done make any kind of sense. "I saw him back there the same as you did. I talked to him. He wanted to come with us, and we left him and his family behind."

She didn't want to believe he was here just to spy on them, or ruin their chances of a fair fight, but it was clearly the case. The only thing she could believe now was that he told the truth, and he hadn't wanted to do it to begin with.

"She's right," Josh said. "It doesn't matter if he was sent here to spy on us or not. If Renzo, or I guess it's Dempsey now, is making threats against his family, that explains everything."

"It explains nothing," Liam said shortly, still glaring at Red. When he took a step forward, Jolie tightened her grip on his arm.

"No, Liam, you don't have to do this."

"I don't care what his reasons are. They don't erase the fact that he came here to hurt you."

"What?" Red's eyes flew wide. He frantically shook his head. "No, I'd never hurt her! I grew up with her! I've known her my whole life! We were friends after you were sent away."

Sort of friends, but Jolie wasn't going to get into the nitty gritty when it looked as if Liam was about to start swinging.

"You are going to tell me absolutely everything Dempsey wanted you to do. That was clearly a message you sent to him."

Red glared at Liam, a growl rising from his throat as he finally decided to stand up for himself. "You mean while I was speaking to my mother and sister who are basically hostages? Yeah, of course that's what it was. I don't want any of you guys hurt, but Jesus Christ, of course I did it! What did you think I was going to do?"

Liam swung. It was fast, so fast Jolie didn't have the chance to try to stop it, and then Red was on the pavement of the gas station parking lot.

There were shouts after that. Jolie looked behind her. Men and women who were filling up their trucks or Subarus with their kids in the back seats stopped what they were doing to look at the fight breaking out.

Jolie shook Liam's arm. "You have to stop. People are watching."

"I should kill you."

Red wiped his mouth with the back of his hand. Josh and Peter moved quickly. "We're starting the engines," Josh said.

Peter nodded. "Hell yeah."

"Liam, we have to get out of here," Jolie said. "If he told Dempsey where we are then he's coming here for us."

Jolie didn't know what Dempsey would want more. To kill Liam or to have her. She didn't care to find out either.

When he didn't look back at her, Jolie shoved him. "Liam!"

Finally, she seemed to catch his attention. Liam looked back at her, his eyes clearing of the rage, but just barely.

"We have to leave."

Liam looked between her and Red on the ground, then back again. Finally, he nodded. "Right."

He reached down, quickly grabbing Red by the throat again. Liam opened the back passenger door of the vehicle he and Jolie shared.

"Hey! Hey, buddy!"

Jolie tensed, looking back. A trucker in a red ball cap came forward, probably at the behest of his wife, because when he got closer and noted how much larger the men over here were than he was, he made sure to keep a healthy distance.

"Everything all right?" he asked, looking to Red.

Red limply waved at him. "Yeah, just dandy."

Liam growled, throwing Red into the back. "Jolie, we have to go."

Jolie snatched her drink off the hood of the SUV before rushing to meet her mate, though she couldn't help but turn back to the concerned citizen. "It's okay! They're friends. He just lost a bet."

She had no idea if the human believed her, but he nodded somewhat vacantly.

Liam quickly pulled her into the back seat with him and Red before slamming the door shut, locking it, and then they were on the move.

The top of Jolie's head itched. She reached up, and then groaned.

Well, she supposed it was a good thing those humans were distracted by Liam punching Red, otherwise she would have given them something else pretty sensational to see since her ears and tail popped out without her noticing.

Which was the least of her worries when, as they drove down the highway, just down the street from the gas station, another truck sped up along side them, rammed into their side, and forced them off the road.

CHAPTER 24

Jolie shrieked. The slush drink she bought literally flew everywhere in an arc of liquid and tiny ice pellets as everything turned to the side and gravity changed, yanking her towards the doors as they went over.

Shouting. Liam called out for her as she went down, saw his hands reaching out for her, as if to protect her from the crash that was about to happen.

He didn't make it in time. She didn't *think* he made it in time, mostly because of the bang, and the way everything went dark.

She couldn't have been passed out for too long. She was still cold from spilling her drink all over herself. The shouting all around her sounded as if it was coming through a tunnel, far away and echoing terribly. Her ears pulsed from the pain of it.

She reached out through the fog for Liam. Where was he? He'd just been in front of her.

"Liam?"

Oh God, what if he wasn't okay? Even an alpha could be hurt in a car wreck.

"Liam."

"I'm right here. I'm here."

His hands. They were the first thing she felt because even though he was right in front of her, she hadn't felt his presence there, not until he'd touched her and she heard his words. Now that she could hear him, she realized he'd been talking to her ever since she woke up. She was just too frazzled, her brain too fried, to have realized it.

Now that he was here, the first thing she wanted was the heat and protection of his body. She curled into him as he pulled her into his arms. She held him tightly. He probably barely felt it, but she couldn't help the panic that had been rushing through her.

"I thought you were hurt," she said, shivering with relief that he apparently wasn't.

He was definitely alive, and he felt strong and whole, and those could only be good signs. She soaked him in, trying desperately to banish the cold grip of terror that had taken her, but even his heat and strength weren't enough to cast it out. Not right away at least.

It was a slow process, though as Liam lifted her into his arms and awkwardly made his way out of the vehicle, she felt it working.

"What happened?"

"The car turned over. You're fine, though, don't worry about anything else."

The anger and rage she'd heard in his voice when Liam had been confronting Red was no longer there. He sounded almost as frazzled as Jolie felt.

The car turned over? What was he talking about?

She tried to look, squinting her eyes to make the scene before her stop spinning and turning, and yeah, even though it felt a lot like she was looking through a reflective, watery surface, that was definitely the SUV she'd been riding in, completely upside down.

Her head totally split when she heard the shouts of the betas. At least they were all right.

"Holy shit! Is she okay?" Jordan asked.

"What the fuck? Is that blood?" Peter sounded more shell shocked than Jolie felt, but at least he could move around.

And what was that about blood?

Jolie lifted her hand to her face, feeling nothing wet there. Liam lowered her wrist, but not before kissing her palm. "Don't think about it, just rest for a bit."

Jolie nodded. She wanted to give him what he wanted, mostly because she felt as if her head was going to explode, but as much as the knock to the back of her head made her want to sleep, there was something else about the situation as a whole that also made that impossible.

Even when she closed her eyes, Jolie couldn't help but hear every single little thing that happened. Her wolf ears were still out, which magnified her hearing even more. The betas around her didn't seem to want to hold still. The sound of the engines of their vehicles were still going loud and strong, and then Liam was suddenly barking orders at them, and he moved quickly when a popping sound went off.

Was that a gun? Jolie groaned, tried to open her eyes, and barely managed to do that.

"What was that sound?"

"Nothing, don't worry about it," Liam said, though his tone was too desperate. He moved too quickly, and it was impossible for Jolie to keep her eyes shut after that.

Liam and the other betas were on the move, running through the trees, abandoning the vehicles they'd taken from Renzo.

And someone was chasing them.

Chasing them and shooting at them.

"You fucking idiot!" Peter yelled. "You're going to hit Jolie! He's holding onto Jolie!"

"Then tell him to drop her and there won't be a problem."

That was Dempsey's voice. Oh no. Dempsey was here? Now? She'd known Red had contacted him, but Dempsey shouldn't have been able to get to them so quickly.

Unless by some fluke he'd already been close by.

Her heart sank.

"You cheating piece of shit!" Jordan yelled. "And you wonder why no one respects you!"

A few more popping sounds. The trees around her rustled.

Oh God, Dempsey really was shooting at them.

"It's only cheating if he comes after me before the moon rises tomorrow. I can do whatever the fuck I want until then," Dempsey called.

He was right, but it did still seem like cheating.

Jolie was with Jordan on this one. He wasn't just an asshole, he really was a piece of shit.

"You can't just carry her like that, Liam," Dempsey called. "You all want to call me a piece of shit, but you all betrayed me for some mutt who uses a woman, an *omega* woman, as a shield. I know who I'd call the piece of shit in that scenario."

Jolie frowned, holding tighter to Liam. What he thought didn't matter to anyone as far as she was concerned.

Surprisingly, it was Red who spoke up, and his voice sounded as if it was coming from their side.

"She's injured! You psychopath! What do you think's going to happen when you run us off the road?"

The fact that Red was on her side, that he hadn't rushed back to Dempsey, was almost enough to make Jolie feel normal again, as if the back of her skull hadn't cracked against the window.

Almost.

There was a brief hesitation from Dempsey. "She's injured?"

"Like you care!" Josh called.

Jolie wished she could see where Dempsey was, but she couldn't. She could only hear. Liam seemed to have hidden them behind some bushes and the roots of a turned over tree.

He didn't shout back to Dempsey, didn't goad him on. Jolie could hear the sound of his heartbeat, and she knew his focus was on her.

"Don't worry about me," she said.

He blinked down at her, then shook his head. "You're the only one I would worry about," he whispered.

"How injured?" Dempsey asked. "Tell me and I'll get an ambulance here if she needs one."

"Like we'd ever trust you!" Franky called.

Jolie was glad to hear it, but the sudden doubt that crept up in Liam's eyes was enough to worry Jolie for sure.

Dempsey didn't shut up either. "Liam, if you really cared, you would let me make that call. I can take care of her like you can't."

"Fuck off!" Red snapped. "You did it to her!"

Dempsey ignored that. "If she has a concussion then she can't go to sleep. Do you even know that? Or does the fact that you never made it past high school keep you from realizing the basics?"

Liam never made it past high school because he'd been banished from the pack, and he'd stayed close for Jolie's sake. Jolie knew that, and she made sure to open her eyes a little wider since she hadn't thought about a possible concussion either. "I'm fine," she mouthed.

Liam nodded, though she could tell he didn't believe her.

This was getting bad. This was getting very bad.

Jolie's wolf ears twitched. She heard more footsteps, circling around. Dempsey had more betas with him. Of course he did. He wouldn't have come alone, and he would have picked people like Red, betas he knew he would be able to control.

Especially after the last time.

"Come on, man, let me help. Tell me how bad is she hurt? Is she bleeding?"

No one answered this time.

"Jolie, if you're awake, call out to me!"

Was he crazy? Why the hell would he ever think she would want to call out to him when he was the one who caused all this trouble to begin with?

Even though she felt like she was high on drugs, she was still in a right frame of mind. She looked up at Liam, and from the expression on his face as he glanced back down at her, he was thinking much the same thing.

Dempsey was a fucking lunatic.

"Jolie!"

"Forget it, Dempsey!" Liam roared. "She's not interested."

"If she dies, it'll be your fault!" Dempsey shrieked back.

If Jolie could have shouted something at him, she would have in an instant. If anything, if she had a brain injury and died, which she doubted at this point, it would be *his* fault, and not Liam's.

She didn't feel anymore pain at all.

"Stay awake." Liam shook her gently, which annoyed her more than anything else at that point. "Don't close your eyes."

"Don't have a concussion," she muttered.

She was pretty sure she didn't have a concussion. It felt right to try to comfort Liam. She didn't want him worrying for her.

He had too much to worry about.

"Is she bleeding? You can at least let me know that much," Dempsey called.

Jolie shook her head, but Liam was looking paler by the second. The golden tan he'd had after years of living out in the wild seemed to vanish before her eyes.

She shook her head. "Not bleeding."

"You are," he mouthed.

What? Jolie frowned. But she wasn't. She would have smelled the blood. Sure, she was a little dizzy and the world around her hadn't quite steadied out, but she was pretty sure she wasn't bleeding or had a concussion.

From the gradual way Liam's expression seemed to become paler, more worried, Jolie got the feeling it wouldn't be up to her whether or not she stayed with him.

"If I surrender to you now," Liam called, " you'll call an ambulance?"

Jolie reached out, grasping at the tight t-shirt over Liam's chest. "No, I'm okay. Don't."

"I've got my phone out right now," Dempsey replied.

None of the other betas said a word. Was that because they were just as shocked as she was? Or because they were getting ready to follow along with the wishes of their alpha?

Jolie didn't know and she didn't care. She was fine. She just needed to snap out of it and stop the dizziness and she could convince him of that.

"Liam, Liam, I'm fine."

Fuck, why did she have to be so tired?

"You will be, I promise," Liam said.

Not good. This was not good.

"I'm coming out," Liam called, and with Jolie still in his arms, he did just that.

CHAPTER 25

Jolie squirmed as much as she was able to in Liam's arms, but it didn't seem to do her any good. Her entire body felt weak, sluggish, and Liam stepped out from the safety of their hiding spot with her.

It was brighter out here, away from their little hidey hole, and Jolie saw them. Dempsey and at least five other betas from the pack. Red wasn't with them, but that was a small comfort, all things considered.

Dempsey actually rushed forward until he was right there, standing in front of Liam, looking down on her as if he had every right to be so close.

"What…?"

"She hit the back of her head." Liam lifted one of his hands. He quickly put it back down around her shoulders, but it wasn't fast enough, and Jolie saw the bright red on his palm.

Did that come from her?

"What happened to her ear?"

Her ear? Oh no. Jolie had the sudden image that one of her wolf ears caught on something and was ripped off, maybe after being sliced on the glass. She'd felt a pinch when everything swirled around her in the SUV, and now she could remember with a sudden, stark clarity that Liam hadn't wanted her touching the top of her head.

"It got cut."

"No shit, it's wide open!" Dempsey shouted, clearly losing his cool.

Which wasn't helping Jolie to keep hers. Her heart slammed.

"What happened?" She looked up at Liam, wanting him to be the one to answer that question for her.

"It's fine," Liam said softly.

"It's not fine! It looks like a cheese string stick that's been pulled apart!"

Jolie's stomach clenched. She was going to be sick.

"Will you shut the fuck up," Liam hissed. "It's not that bad and all she needs is some stitches and to keep the ear out while it heals."

"Yeah, great, it'll be *super* easy to get her treated at a hospital with this."

"I'm sure you'll figure something out if you really gave a shit."

Liam continued to growl and grumble, but it wasn't until he handed Jolie over to Dempsey that she reached out for him.

"No, no, what are you doing?"

Dempsey wouldn't give her back. Liam had to know that.

"I'll come for you later, after we settle this," Liam promised, then he growled. "I can trust that you're going to keep your filthy hands to yourself until she recovers?"

"Jesus Christ! What the hell do you think I am? I'm not

some perv who would molest my mate when she's barely conscious."

Jolie was glad to hear that, because she wouldn't have given Dempsey that kind of trust just a minute ago. All the same, she didn't want to go with him. She wanted to stay with Liam. She didn't want to leave his side and she felt fine enough to stay.

She reached for him, tried to take him by the hand, but she couldn't seem to grasp onto his fingers. "Liam,"

"It's all right," Liam promised. "Everything's going to be okay. He'll get you to a hospital, and we'll settle this."

Dempsey handed Jolie over to one of his betas. She knew this man, the same way she knew the betas who had defected to Liam. She tried to look up at him, to meet his eyes and tell him she didn't want to be with Dempsey, but maybe her garbled words weren't enough to convince him that betraying his current alpha was a good idea, because the beta barely took the time to look down at her.

"I'll fight you man to man after she's safe in the hospital," Liam said. Jolie didn't have to look at him to know he was clenching his fists. "Then it'll be just you and me, and we can settle this where she won't get hurt."

"We *could* do that," Dempsey said.

Jolie glanced to her mate just as Dempsey lifted his hand. Another loud popping noise went off. Jolie flinched from the sound, so close to her, and the small puff of smoke that came from the end of the gun.

Liam ducked out of the way, but it was too late. It was almost as if she watched the entire thing happen in slow motion, and the sudden puncture of metal against flesh, the spatter of blood, were the first things Jolie noticed as Liam went down, quickly rolled back to his feet, but then swayed as he clutched at his side.

Bright red spilled between his tight fingers. Jolie couldn't breathe. She could hardly think.

Dempsey shot Liam. It was like being sucker punched, but worse because Liam had stepped out for her, so Dempsey would call an ambulance for her.

"Alpha," said one of the betas on Dempsey's side.

Apparently, the act had stunned them, too.

"Liam!" Jolie struggled to push herself out of the arms of the beta. She almost managed it, but the man pulled himself together quickly enough, keeping her from rolling out of his arms before she could get anywhere.

Liam's betas quickly rushed out of their own hiding places and surrounded their alpha protectively. Red stood with them, looking mightily unsure of himself, but he was there.

Dempsey shook his head. "Nuh uh, you get your ass over here."

Red looked to Liam, and then back at Dempsey. His gaze briefly landed on Jolie, and she could see the small war going on within him. She knew what he was going to do.

What he had to do.

Red slowly, carefully, walked back over to Dempsey's side. Dempsey gave the man a hard slap upside the head when he got close enough. It was hard enough that Jolie winced on impact, and Red stumbled down to his knees. Maybe slapped was the wrong way to put it. With the way that looked, it was more as if Red got punched upside the head.

"Cowardly bitch," Jordan muttered.

Red flinched. "I can't—"

"I wasn't talking to you," Jordan snapped, and then he sneered at Dempsey.

Dempsey shrugged. "Yeah, well I learned my lesson after you all betrayed me for a stray dog."

Dempsey lifted his weapon and pulled the trigger one more time. Jordan's head pulled back, as if someone had thrown their fist and made impact right between his eyes.

Only it was worse than that, and even the betas standing behind Dempsey shouted when Jordan went down, his body dropping, blood spilling from between his eyes.

"Jesus Christ!" Peter fell to his knees beside Jordan. Jolie could hardly breathe as she watched, praying, even though she already knew the answer she would get.

Jordan would never survive a gunshot to the head.

Liam roared, his fangs popping out of his mouth, fur sprouting around his body until he looked like the wolf man.

"*Motherfucker!*"

"Yeah, whatever," Dempsey said, though his hand trembled as he raised his weapon one more time, pointing it between Liam's eyes.

Jolie's heart flew into her throat. "*No!*"

Peter lunged in front of his alpha, shielding Liam with his body, but the gun did nothing more than click.

The magazine was empty, and there were no bullets in the chamber.

Jolie didn't understand right away, not until after Dempsey pulled the trigger again in an attempt to make the gun fire, as if he thought it was just an error and the gun would go off if he tried again. It didn't, proving the chamber wasn't clogged, he didn't have a blank bullet, or whatever else could cause a loaded weapon to not fire. It was just empty.

Jolie finally breathed. Peter cringed, stepping away from his alpha, looking up at him, and then down at himself, as if to confirm there was nothing wrong with him, and he wasn't bleeding all over the place.

Or dying.

"Holy shit," he said through a harsh breath. "Oh fuck, I'm alive."

Dempsey hardly seemed to notice. He was more focused on the fact that his weapon was out of bullets.

The empty magazine dropped from the handle, and when he reached into his back pocket, presumably for another one, Liam didn't hesitate.

He rushed forward, his hands, and claws, reaching out for Dempsey's throat.

The world was still spinning from the bang to the back of her head, but Jolie could swear she saw the full force of Liam's inner wolf come forward, powerful and strong.

And angry.

Dempsey screamed like a little girl when Liam grabbed him and they went down.

None of his betas helped him, though Jolie paid attention. Some stepped forward, looked amongst each other, then stopped. It was as if they themselves didn't know what the right thing to do was. They were stuck, but they'd also watched their alpha shoot and kill a young beta.

Decision apparently made, no one moved to help Dempsey as he struggled to ward Liam off.

"Get him off me! Get him off!" he shrieked, sounding more and more like he was losing control, like he was panicking.

Liam was fully in his wolf form, and he towered over Dempsey's body, his engorged teeth crushing the muscle and bone of Dempsey's forearm in a nasty, wet crunch while Dempsey kicked at the wolf that had him.

He wasn't going anywhere. Jolie could see that. Dempsey had betrayed the last shred of goodwill Liam had for him when he caused the crash that hurt Jolie, made such a dishonorable move, and then kill one of his betas.

The youngest beta of their group.

Dempsey was a dead man, and even though no one moved to help either of them, the aura from the men around her was thick and intoxicating. Vengeance, anger, the need to make a wrong right again was right there and at the forefront of everyone's eyes.

Even if it wouldn't bring Jordan back, no one was going to let Dempsey get out of this alive. Dempsey handed over the control of his own betas to Liam with that move, and now Liam would solidify it by taking Dempsey out.

After enough kicking in the throat and face, Dempsey finally got a good enough shot in on Liam's eye, forcing him to release Dempsey's arm.

It didn't distract Liam for long, his bloody lips pulling back, revealing long red and white teeth. His nose scrunched up, and he was by far the most terrifying thing Jolie had ever seen.

The same was apparently true for Dempsey. He scrambled back, desperate to find his gun and the magazine clip in the pine needles and weeds.

"Help me, you idiots!" he screeched.

"We obey our alpha. No one else," said the beta holding Jolie.

She looked up at him. He glanced down at her, and then turned his attention to Liam. "I can call for the ambulance, if one of the humans from the gas station didn't already."

"No," Jolie muttered, blinking wide. "I need...I need to be here for this."

Her tongue felt thick in her mouth. She hoped that was just something she felt in her head and wasn't real, otherwise she might be in trouble.

The oversized wolf that was her mate looked up at her. His eyes flashed, a bright silver color, the color of a full moon.

"You can't challenge me now!" Dempsey shrieked. "It's not the full moon! It won't be a legal take over! You have to wait!"

"I don't think it matters too much at this point," Red said, his tone soft, almost dead.

"Shut the fuck up! Don't forget for one second that your mother and sister are still back on pack territory."

"Yes," Red said softly, turning away from Jordan's body so he could face Dempsey. "And soon my new alpha will be there to set them free."

That seemed to be the sentence that made it click for Dempsey how much trouble he was in. His eyes changed. There was a panic and fear in them that Jolie had never seen on anyone before. She didn't think she'd ever seen a look like that even in a movie. It was kind of crazy.

Dempsey turned back to the large silver wolf stalking towards him. He clutched his bleeding arm, continuously backing away, desperate to put any kind of distance between himself and the animal creeping closer and closer towards hm.

Jolie wanted to look away. She didn't know if she could watch Liam kill him, but every time she tried to look away from Dempsey, she only saw Jordan.

It was better to look at Dempsey when Liam lunged at him, mouth wide open, fangs at the ready, and hear that brief scream before Liam's teeth closed in around Dempsey's throat.

Miraculously, Dempsey managed to raise both of his arms to ward off the teeth. Jolie held her breath, watching Dempsey's body tremble as he struggled to hold back those teeth. Some of them punctured his arms. Jolie saw the teeth piercing through his clothes and skin. More blood spattered across Dempsey's face and Liam's wet nose.

Dempsey's cheeks turned a bright shade of red, and not because of the blood that was getting on him. The strain was too much. He was clearly struggling to hold back the teeth, as if he was fighting against keeping a living bear trap from snapping shut on his neck.

It wasn't going to happen. He was screwed.

And then it did happen. Dempsey, face red, body trembling from the effort, released a hard roar just before the bear trap snapped shut.

Then silence.

CHAPTER 26

Jolie puked. She couldn't help it. Watching the life get crunched out of Dempsey's neck, listening to that wet noise, seeing and smelling the blood, so much blood, was too much.

It wasn't just the blood. The acidic smell of urine as Dempsey pissed himself in fear, and then let everything else go in death, combined to create a cocktail of dank body fluids and she just couldn't keep it down.

Her head throbbed. The damned ground beneath her wouldn't stop swerving and turning, and now the pain combined with the death and blood...

She couldn't help it.

The beta holding her stumbled back, swore.

Jolie apologized for vomiting on his shoes, but she couldn't help herself and then did it again immediately after.

Eventually, someone else came and she was pushed into the arms of another beta.

Looking up, she noticed it was Red. He turned away, giving his back to what Liam was doing with Dempsey's body. She was pretty sure he was eating some of it, lost to the wild nature of his wolf form.

"You don't need to see that," Red said.

Jolie nodded.

There was also something about drinking some of the blood, or eating a bit of the flesh of the previous alpha when doing a takeover like this.

She hoped he wasn't taking a lot. She didn't like the idea of Liam eating any part of another person.

"Is my ear really bad?"

"No," Red said, his eyes scanning her wolf ears. "It's bloody, but just cut in a couple of places. I think Dempsey was being an idiot, and Liam was just overly worried. You could probably let them sink back into your body and they'd probably heal on their own. I think you need to get your head checked, though."

"For a concussion?"

"Yeah."

There were lights. Flashing lights. They were enough to give her a headache.

Then she realized what they were, and what the sounds were that came with them.

Sirens. Red and blue. Police lights.

Holy shit.

"I guess one of the humans called the police. Looks like a firetruck and ambulance are here for you." Red smiled down at her. "Aren't you special?"

"I want to stay with Liam."

"I know, but do us a favor and don't mention his name while you're getting your head checked out. Just say you can't remember anything after the crash. We'll get Liam out of here and make up some story about a bear that ran Dempsey off the side of the road."

They made this decision for the sake of their alpha, and

for Jolie, all on their own. Just the way a team of loyal betas should.

For a split second, Jolie didn't feel quite so horrible anymore. She felt as if she could get up and start dancing around.

As much as she wanted to stay with Liam and make sure everything would be all right, she was glad just knowing he was going to be well cared for by a group of loyal betas.

Maybe she dozed off after that, because it seemed as if she blinked before she was put on a stretcher.

"She flew out the window. She landed way over there!" Red said.

"Does she have any allergies?"

"No, I don't think so."

She didn't. Her ears and tail must have melted back into her body as well because she didn't hear any shocked gasps from the paramedics as they took her away to the hospital.

"Stay awake. Look at me. How many fingers am I holding up?"

Jolie blinked, and she did her best to do everything these people wanted from her while they worked on her.

If Liam was going to go to Renzo and let him know what had happened, taking command of the pack as the rightful alpha, then Jolie needed to do her best to recover so she could be by his side when that happened.

* * *

JOLIE HAD NEVER SPENT a lot of time in a hospital before. There was once when she was a little girl, still living with Liam and his parents, when she fell from a tree and needed quick stitches on the back of her leg, but that was about it.

Being a werewolf, omega or otherwise, usually meant that staying long term in a hospital was something of a mistake. It rarely happened unless absolutely necessary, and the few times it did, a beta, or the alpha himself, would sometimes follow the sick or injured shifter just to make sure nothing happened with the blood work.

Or that any accidental transformations were covered up.

The fact that she was in the hospital by herself, with no one watching over her, was incredibly weird. The beeping noises, the strong, sterile scent, coupled with the depressing coughs that came from patients in the other rooms, all created an air of loneliness around her that she couldn't shake.

Ultimately, Jolie was glad for it. Even though she hated the way the nurses forced her to stay awake, rarely letting her close her eyes for more than a few minutes before gently shaking her shoulder. At least it meant that the betas were watching over Liam, protecting him, the way they should be, instead of focusing their attention on her.

So long as she was here, it meant Liam could be protected by his betas.

It didn't stop her from wanting to see him. Desperately.

She'd hoped to be taken out of the hospital that night, but it didn't happen. She spent the whole night, barely catnapping, trying not to scratch at the bandages that were wrapped around the back of her head.

It itched, though it was also possible that the bandages were keeping her ears down whenever they tried to come back out again.

That might explain the itching.

Her heart ached, too. Ached to know what was happening with Liam, with the pack. There was no way in hell Jordan's death could be played off as happening from a car wreck, especially so far from the road. They would have taken his body. Had they had a funeral for him yet? God, what about his family? The betas who followed Liam took a great risk, one that Red wasn't willing to pay, but she couldn't imagine Jordan thought he might get killed.

She hadn't thought Dempsey would have been the type to do that.

Most alphas had to kill at one point or another. Sometimes it was just, and Jolie wasn't old enough to know if Liam's father had ever been forced into that situation, but she knew he hadn't been the type to simply execute another man like that.

A young beta who had so much to give. He was gone because Dempsey had wanted to make a point.

She was glad he was dead. She wished she could have helped Liam do it. Every time she dozed, she dreamed about it, though in her dreams, she kept trying to fix it. She kept whispering to Jordan to not get too close. Jolie told the betas that Dempsey had one more bullet left in his gun, anything to undo what happened.

The only problem was the nurses kept waking her up.

It was morning when someone came for her to check her out. Josh was the first to show up, apparently pretending to be her older brother.

"I hear you had a good night's sleep."

Jolie glared at him as the nurses helped her into a wheelchair after letting her get dressed in the clothes she'd arrived in. She would have flipped him off, but it didn't seem right in this place.

Her clothes had been cleaned, which was good, but Jolie wasn't detecting any scent of her mate on them anymore, which was bad. The lack of that small connection, scent, which was the one sense that stuck with people for longer than their memory of sight, bugged the ever-loving hell out of her.

She wanted to ask, wanted to grab Josh by the collar of that brown leather jacket he wore, yank him down, growl, and demand he answer every single question she had about what the hell was going on.

It was honestly the biggest lesson in patience for her as Josh signed her out, calmly speaking with the nurse at the front desk, and then wheeled her to the front sliding doors.

It was only when fresh air touched her face that Jolie allowed herself to speak. "You'd better have some good news for me."

Josh helped her stand. "Yeah, sort of," Josh said. "We can talk more in the car. How are you feeling about Red?"

"Red?" Jolie's bandages were still on. Had they not been, her wolf ears might've popped out. "Why? What happened?"

"Well, he's driving us to meet with Liam."

"He is? Liam didn't send him away?" And then the more important question stuck in her mind. "Why didn't Liam come to get me? Is this the part where you start explaining to me the bad news?"

"Sort of, but don't worry, everything's fine. The police, and pretty much the entire surrounding area, are out looking for a killer bear, the one that took out Dempsey."

A black SUV stopped in front of them. Josh reached out, opening the back passenger door for her.

Jolie didn't take her eyes away from Josh. "And?"

Josh sighed. "And, ever since you were brought to the hospital last night, Liam's been stuck in his wolf form. We're hiding him as best we can," he said quickly. "But we think it might help if you were there to calm him down. He's still acting a little...on the wild side."

That couldn't be good.

With renewed strength, Jolie pulled herself into the back seat. Red was in the front, and he was indeed driving. He glanced back at her, a sorry expression on his face that she had no time to feel any pity for.

"How are you feeling?"

Jolie nodded. "I'll be better when you get me to Liam. Is he still planning on taking over the pack?"

Red shrugged as Josh pulled himself into the passenger seat up front. "We think so, either way, after the rest of the pack hears what Dempsey did, they won't defect to Renzo. It'll be his anyway, regardless of how he took Dempsey out."

"We just have to get this done quickly," Josh said, glancing back at her. "Renzo's been blowing up Dempsey's phone with calls and texts. If he hasn't already figured out what's happened, then he will soon."

"You're worried Renzo will do something rash?"

Rash seemed to be the nice way of putting it. She could just imagine what was on the minds of these betas. Namely the horrible things that could happen to their families if they didn't get back and let everyone know what had happened.

Their silence was enough.

"Right, okay, take me to Liam."

CHAPTER 27

*L*uckily, there was something in the car for the mild headache Jolie still had, and on the ride to wherever it was Liam was being hidden, she was extra grateful to note her dizziness wasn't coming back. That likely meant her balance wasn't all that affected anymore either. Jolie wasn't much use to Liam if she wasn't at her best, and she remembered all the things the nurses warned her about when she'd left the hospital.

There wasn't much that could be done about the stress of the situation. Not when it came to her mate. She'd been separated from Liam for too many years. Jolie could hardly get control over herself just thinking about the state he was in now.

Jolie scratched the side of her arm, then clutched her hands together, needing something to do with them.

"Don't be nervous," Red said. "We've been taking good care of him, and he hasn't *completely* lost it."

When Josh didn't say anything sarcastic to that, Jolie knew she could trust Red's assessment. As much as she was able to, at any rate. "I need to see him for myself. Until then…" She trailed off. She didn't know what else she could say.

In her head, she pictured Liam totally lost to the wild animal of his wolf. If that happened, would he be able to come back from it? Some shifters chose to stay in their wolf shapes for their entire lives. Some got lost to the wild animal within them.

Liam never gave her the impression that he struggled with holding that side of himself back. Jolie didn't even know what it felt like to fight off those kinds of urges as an omega. The only thing she had trouble fighting off was keeping her ears and tail hidden away whenever she got nervous or excited about something.

"I promise he's fine," Josh said. They turned off the highway and down onto a dirt road. "He's just…antsy."

Jolie blinked. "Meaning what? Can he understand anything you're saying? Is he responding to anything?"

"Well, he is, sort of," Josh said, and then he and Red unhelpfully looked at each other, as if they were both nervous about telling her anything more.

"I mean, he hasn't run off to go find you, or anyone else, which is good," Red finished, adding, "We were worried he'd run after you at the hospital when he looked up and seemed to realize you weren't there. Peter and Franky nearly got bitten trying to hold him back."

Was it bad that Jolie felt warm by that admission? Probably a little bad. She hoped neither beta up front would look into the rearview mirror and see her blushing like this.

"Thank you for keeping him safe." Jolie reached to the front seat, grasping Red's shoulder. "Both of you."

Red pressed his lips together. He didn't say anything to her after that. She got an idea of what, or who, he was thinking of in that moment. When this was all over, she would take the time to mourn for Jordan. Until then, Liam was her focus, getting to him and calming him down so he could be presentable for the rest of the pack.

They stopped after what seemed like an eternity of driving, though looking at the clock, it was barely fifteen minutes from the hospital to where they were now.

A clearing opened up along the narrow dirt road, and what looked to be an old cabin.

The kind Jolie wouldn't want to stay in to save her life. The roof was actually missing, and it sagged sadly to the side, as though it was a dying plant.

Or also mourning all the death and blood that happened last night.

They brought Liam *here*? It was as depressing as an abandoned graveyard. How was he supposed to recover and get back to himself when these were his surroundings?

At first, she figured Liam might be inside it that wilted building, but no, the second the SUV came to a stop, from behind the falling over, rotting cabin, an oversized gray wolf appeared, standing at attention, ears flicking, and staring suspiciously at the vehicle.

Despite being in his wolf form, he looked all right. He didn't look as if he was injured, no signs of a limp, and none of the fur she could see was dark and matted down with blood.

Jolie jumped out of the passenger door. She ran to her mate.

"Liam!"

Those ears flicked again. Liam didn't run back to her. He let her come to him.

The betas, all of whom kept a healthy distance from the wolf, were too late to stop her before she could throw her arms around the wide neck of her mate. With his sheer size, and the protective fur around his throat, she was unable to loop her arms all the way around him, but that didn't matter.

He was here. He was warm and alive. Whether he was having trouble controlling his inner wild side or not, she would deal with that later.

"I missed you so much. I'm sorry I wasn't there last night." God, no wonder he'd lost control. All the blood, losing Jordan right in front of him, and getting shot, of course it would take its toll.

And she'd been resting peacefully in a hospital bed. A concussion seemed like nothing compared to what Liam and the betas had been going through.

"I'm so sorry."

Her hands searched. Reminded that he'd been shot, she searched for the wound. It would be on his midsection, but the fur on him was blocking her view of it.

Jolie pulled back, looking at the betas around her. "Where's his gunshot wound? Did anyone treat him?"

Franky shrugged helplessly, the bags under his eyes dark and heavy. "We tried. He's not letting any of us near him anymore."

"We think he's okay, though," Mitch added. "We did manage to get him cleaned up in one of the streams, when he was letting us close. I think the bullet's still inside him."

Jolie blinked. "You mean the wound *healed* around it?" She looked back up at Liam. "We have to get it out of him!"

"It's not a silver bullet," Josh said, scratching the back of his head. "We can take it out if he wants it out, but it's not happening until you can get him to shift."

Liam's wet nose sniffed at the top of Jolie's head. She looked up at her mate. He looked down at her, his eyes wide and bright, each one the size of her fist. She was pretty sure he was in there. There was certainly nothing wild and savage about the way he sniffed at her, his head butting against her shoulder, as though begging for a good scratch behind his ears.

Jolie couldn't resist giving it to him.

Liam often said how soft her wolf ears were. She thought the same about his.

"So long as you're okay, then I guess it's fine." Jolie needed to learn more about what could happen if a bullet was left inside someone's body. She didn't like the idea of it being in there, but there wasn't much she could do about it in the moment. "Liam, come on, you can understand me, right? I'm sorry I had to go to the hospital for a bit, and for what happened to Jordan, but I'm fine now. I'm right here and everything will be okay."

Those eyes flashed once more. Jolie's heart jumped.

Recognition. That's what she saw in his gaze. He recognized her. He *had* to.

"We need to get back to the pack, to let everyone know what happened to Dempsey and Jordan. They won't follow you if you show you can't control yourself." Jolie scrubbed her fingers through the coarser, thicker fur around Liam's neck. The deeper down into his coat she went, the softer his fur became. She hoped her touch had all the right effects she was looking for. Comfort, familiarity. She inched closer still, wanting her mate to take in more of her scent.

Scent was the strongest sense for a shifter, for anyone, after all.

"Come back to me."

He did. It took some doing, but it finally seemed to happen. Jolie felt the ripple in Liam's fur and muscles before she saw any outward changes. The sounds of bones snapping, the way Liam's body shrank down, fur shedding in some places, and in others sinking back into his pores, made Jolie's heart leap as the human version of her mate appeared before her.

Liam gasped for breath when he was in complete human form. He leaned heavily against Jolie's body. She curled her arms around him to keep him standing. Without her there, he might have fallen to his knees.

Jolie pressed her forehead to Liam's chest. The pulse of his heartbeat thudded against her skin.

"So glad you're back," she gasped. She might start shivering in much the same way he was right now.

"Could say the same for you," Liam replied, his grip on her tightening, and she felt his want for her, his relief, and his love.

She'd known he'd be worried about her. Jolie stamped down the little feeling of glee that thought left her with. Yeah, it was childish and stupid. She knew her mate loved her and cared for her and all those other good things, but the little telltale signs that proved it still made her happy. "I was fine. They just wouldn't let me sleep last night, that's all." She would have to be watched as she slept tonight, but she would give her mate that news after everything was finished. "Your betas took good care of you."

Liam released a low, rumbling noise deep in his chest, even as Red stepped forward and put his long duster jacket over Liam's naked body. "They shouldn't have to care for me."

"They're your betas." Jolie took the jacket by the collar, straightening it around Liam's shoulders. "It's what they're supposed to do."

Liam grunted a short noise, still appearing mightily unconvinced, but he did look back at the betas who surrounded him, the men who had left the pack to follow Liam, and the ones who were now at his side only because Dempsey had showed his true hand. "Thank you," Liam said, and then turned away from them, his mouth tightening.

Jolie smiled. She ran her fingers through his short, sweat-damp hair. "You'll get used to other people watching out for you soon enough." She had every intention of making sure of that.

Liam nodded. His betas grinned and elbowed each other. The ones who had most recently stood behind Dempsey still appeared unsure of their place.

Liam ignored them and looked up to the sky. "How long until sundown?"

"Not for another six hours," Josh said quickly. "Lots of time to get you cleaned up and looking good for when we put you in front of Renzo."

Jolie was most curious about this part. It wasn't as if she'd ever been personally involved in any pack take overs. "Do you think Renzo can take the pack over for himself now that Dempsey is gone?"

Liam's brow pulled together. He shook his head. "No, he gave up control over the pack, and if he did try to take it over again, I think he knows I would fight him for it, and win."

"The pack won't follow him after this anyway," Franky said, threading his fingers together and cracking his knuckles. "I bet they were pissed off to all hell and back with just what happened to Red's family, then there are our families, and then Jordan's." The easy-going smile left Franky's face at the mention of Jordan.

Jolie's heart clenched as if there was a clawed, bony fist squeezing the life out of it. She had to take in a deep breath just to get herself back under control. Her eyes burned just thinking about.

It was…too damned fresh. She couldn't let herself get caught up in that right now.

"We'll see how it goes when we get there." Liam's eyes blazed a bright shade of red. "I should kill Renzo anyway."

No one said anything to that. The silence was heavy, though not because Jolie got the impression the betas would hold it against Liam for not being able to hold himself back.

More as if they were on his side, and wouldn't be able to blame him if he went through with it.

"We'll find another place to stay until you recover," Josh said. "Or we can stay here. Either way, we'll make sure you're strong enough to go back to the pack looking like a king coming home."

Jolie's spine felt a little straighter at those words. They fit so perfectly, because they were true. Liam was the prodigal son coming home, and she was honored to be at his side when he made his final confrontation with Renzo.

Liam nodded. "I'm going to need a couple of minutes, some water to wash the taste of Dempsey from my mouth, and then I'll be ready."

"We've still got bottled water in the cars, Alpha," Mitch said quickly, and he rushed over to get them.

Liam gave Jolie one last quick look before following his beta.

Jolie would join him in a minute. She just had to ask Josh about something before he scrambled off to help his alpha prepare as well.

"Hey, mind if I ask you about something?"

Josh blinked. "Yeah, sure, but I need to get this place cleaned up. We can't leave any traces we were here."

Jolie looked around. The dead atmosphere gave her the impression that was the last thing he needed to worry about, and aside from a few footprints in the dirt and sand, there wasn't much to show anyone living had been here in some years.

Unless there was something else he was worried about leaving traces of behind.

"What did you do with Jordan?"

Josh's entire expression sank. "We, uh, wrapped him up in some of our jackets. There were also some towels in the back of the SUV, but it's not really the same."

"You didn't bury him here, did you?" The thought of Jordan being alone here, underground in this depressing place, made her shudder.

"No, we're going to try bringing him home to his parents for a proper funeral, but we can't leave him here for too long. We didn't want to leave him in the vehicle we brought because we didn't want, well, his body to heat up."

"Where is he?"

"Around back. We found a nice bed of grass and some flowers to set him on for now."

She was shocked to find out there were flowers growing around here. She hadn't noticed them when she'd arrived.

"Thank you for what you did," Jolie said softly, having no idea what else to say.

Josh nodded, though he didn't answer. The topic was something clearly hard for both of them to swallow.

Jolie felt the need to continue, to fill the silence with words, as if that would make it less horrible somehow. "I'm grateful you guys were taking care of Liam while I was away, but I had to wonder about this place."

Josh stared at her as if he was confused. "Were you worried some humans would show up? We didn't catch any scents of people around here."

"Not exactly that." Jolie looked over at the cabin itself, tried to think of a nice way to suggest bringing Liam, when half wild and in his wolf form, to a place where a nest of crazed opossums with rabies could be hiding out wasn't the best idea, and realized she couldn't think of a nice way to put it at all. It was bad enough Jordan's body was lying in the back when there could be pests sniffing around him, looking for a meal.

She groaned.

"Oh," Josh laughed a little. "Yeah, we thought you might

notice that, and don't worry, we chased away the raccoons before Liam could see them and chase them himself."

"I thought I smelled something." Raccoons weren't much better than opossums, as far as she was concerned.

"But other than that, we thought you might appreciate it. It's nice here. We thought all these flowers around would calm him down, maybe remind him a little of you. Kind of romantic when we brought you back to him."

Jolie's eyes popped wide. "Romantic?"

"Yeah." Josh looked at her, scratching the back of his head. "I know it's not exactly the best scene, considering everything, but, we all just thought…I don't know."

Jolie had to have another look, and this time, without the intense dread clouding her mind and heart, she *was* able to see a little of what Josh saw.

"I mean, all things considered, I guess we would have taken anywhere as a safe hiding spot, but when we found this, close to the hospital and all, it just seemed perfect."

Jolie nodded. He was right. It was.

The cabin itself might've been too dangerous for anyone to actually use, what with the way it sagged as if its four walls were about to give out if a small bird so much as sat on top of the structure, but the bright green moss growing along the outer edges of the decaying wood added a pretty highlight to the scene. Tiny white and yellow flowers bloomed in the few patches of green that sprouted along the ground around the cabin itself, like happy little gnomes congregating in their favorite place for a party.

A few of those tiny buds even sprouted from the moss on the cabin itself.

A Goddamned butterfly, of all things, floated passed the scene, giving it more of a mythical, airy appeal.

It could have been a painting. It was that pretty.

Jolie felt bad about calling this place a graveyard. Jordan would have liked it here. If he could see it.

Suddenly, she needed to get back to her mate. She needed to see him, touch him, hold him, and to let herself feel the gratitude she needed over the fact that he was alive.

"Thanks, Josh." Jolie turned away from him, quickly clearing her throat, and rushing off to find her mate as her eyes burned.

She found him standing with Mitch and Franky behind the SUV she'd been driven here in, with a hard scowl on his face, a half full water bottle in one hand, wiping the back of his mouth with the other. His attention was focused solely on her the second she made her appearance, the scowl melting off his face as she immediately went into his arms.

Liam's body didn't tense. He was immediately open and pliant to her, his body accepting her in his space. "Are you all right?" His hand stroked through her hair, over the bandage still wrapped around her head.

Jolie nodded, and held him just a little bit tighter. "I am now."

CHAPTER 28

Getting back home, to the pack where Jolie grew up, a small pack of betas behind her, and her mate, the most powerful alpha she knew, beside her, wasn't the joyous occasion Jolie had fantasized it would be.

The fact that Jordan was still dead, his body wrapped up in the back of the SUV, being carefully guarded by Red and Peter, made it something of a solemn affair. It wasn't like it had been outside that decaying cabin, where Jolie had first seen one image of it, and then the next when Josh explained to her why they were satisfied with their choice of hiding place.

The trees hanging low over the road leading onto pack territory seemed to slump a little more than she remembered; the colors of the grass, even the flowers, were dull, and the weeds seemed to have taken over since she'd last made her appearance as Renzo's guest.

Everyone was still there, however. All the faces Jolie recognized appeared along the side of the road as they drove back onto pack territory, as if they had been waiting anxiously for the return of Dempsey.

Or their new alpha.

"Oh God," Jolie groaned, looking at all the faces, the small homes behind them. She didn't see Jordan's parents yet, but she saw the house where he'd lived with them. It was a small place, a cube with a triangle roof, but the vegetable garden out front that his mother tended was still there.

She only cared for it because of Jordan, because she wanted him to always have food on the table even when times were rough. Jolie knew because she'd spent a few nights on their couch after Liam's parents were killed.

Would she still care for it? Now that her only child was gone?

Liam's arm looped around Jolie's shoulders, holding her tight. "That's not on you," he said softly, leaning down so his mouth was closer to her ear. "I'll be the one to tell them. I'll take the blame for this."

Jolie shook her head. "No, you can't. It's not…I'm the one who did this."

If she hadn't run off, if she hadn't tried to convince any of the betas to follow Liam…he might still be alive.

Liam was silent for a moment, thoughtful. "Then we'll both carry that load, but I'll be the one who tells them, and I'll let them take their anger out on me. Don't argue," he said when she opened her mouth. "I'm the alpha. It's right that this falls to me."

Jolie snapped her mouth shut just then, realizing that, essentially, he was right. A good alpha always took responsibility for the failings of his pack. She hadn't ever stopped to think about that when she'd done her best to convince Liam to come back to the pack. She'd only thought about the good that could come from it. Never the bad, never the uncomfortable, and even horrible duties Liam would be saddled with.

From the silence in the rest of the vehicle, the betas were thinking much the same thing.

Renzo appeared before Josh had the chance to kill the engine, exiting the home that used to belong to Liam and his parents, and would belong to him again.

Jolie, Liam, and the betas who had all been squeezed into the SUV exited it. Peter had actually been riding on the roof. Good thing the drive hadn't been long.

For the first time in a long time, Renzo hardly looked as if he belonged there. She couldn't pin down what it was that gave her that impression of weakness around him. He still walked with his shoulders back, his head held high, his clothes pressed and clean…so what was it?

The almost anemic appearance of his cheeks and throat? The firm press of his colorlesss lips? His clenched fists didn't give off the impression of power either. He looked like an old man walking towards a beheading when he stood before Liam.

He at least tried to give off the impression of some sort of control as he looked up at him. "Dempsey isn't here."

"I know." Liam nodded.

The silence from the surrounding pack was thick. Stale marshmallow thick.

Renzo's gaze flicked up and down Liam's naked body. Liam had removed the long duster he'd been offered before. He'd said he didn't need to wear it if he was going to shift again. Jolie could just imagine Renzo was thinking those same things.

"Did you kill him?"

"Only after he shot me in the gut." Liam pointed to the small, healing pink scar that had closed over the wound. She still wanted that bullet out of him, but she didn't think that would be happening any time soon.

Renzo growled, some color finally returning to his cheeks. "You killed him."

"Yeah." Liam nodded. "And I'm hoping you give me a reason to kill you right now."

A shriek sounded. Jolie took her eyes away from her mate and former alpha, noting the way Jordan's mother appeared, rushing towards the wrapped body Mitch and Franky unloaded from the back seat.

Jordan's mother was only held back when his father quickly wrapped his mate up into his arms, stopping her from grabbing onto the corpse when she was in such a state. Jolie's throat closed as she cried, sinking to the ground, her husband coming with her while Josh stepped up to them to explain what had happened.

Liam spoke louder. "You didn't want to face me like an alpha, so you handed control of the pack over to Dempsey and sent him out to get at us with a gun. It didn't work, and now Jordan is dead. You're damn right I killed Dempsey. I killed him and drank his damned blood yesterday, and I don't give a shit about full moon rituals."

It was clear he was speaking to the rest of the pack, even though he wasn't taking his eyes away from Renzo.

"Anyone who will follow me is welcome to. Anyone still loyal to you or Dempsey can get the fuck off my lawn."

Jolie shivered. The power of Liam's voice vibrated through her, and it was more than just because he was her mate and alpha. He could be a perfect stranger, a man she'd never met before today, and somehow, she got the feeling his tone, his body, and his eyes, would still be calling out for her obedience.

And she would willingly give it to him. Even if she had no idea who Liam was, the commanding air around him called to her on an instinctual level. It was almost enough to make her howl for him again. She might have if the situation wasn't so damned serious.

The problem was the silence around the rest of the pack. Some people stared pityingly down at Jordan's parents, others stared with relief at their own sons, the betas who had come back with Liam alive and well.

Generally, everyone seemed to be in major shock.

Jolie stepped up to her mate. She reached out, grasping onto his much larger hand, threading her fingers through his. She kept her back straight and stared defiantly up at Renzo. If they were going to do this, then they were going to do it as one. The new alpha would have his mate beside him, combining her strength with his, showing her support.

Renzo didn't glare down at her. Jolie half expected him to, but he didn't. The way he barely acknowledged her seemed worse than a simple glare.

"Well?" Liam snapped.

Renzo shrugged. "Not really up to me anymore. I'm not the alpha. Just a matter if the pack wants to follow you. Standing there naked like a warrior alpha of the old days might seem great, but you don't even have a full high school education. If they won't follow you, that's not their fault."

Liam growled, showing off his teeth.

Jolie clenched his hand. He stopped quickly.

"I would follow him," Jolie said, loud enough that she hoped the rest of the pack was paying attention.

Renzo nodded. "Great. That's one." He lifted his index finger, as if she needed it. "Any others?"

"Me." Red stood up. He stepped away from the sidelines, where he'd been standing with an older woman and young girl. His mother and sister. "I'll follow him and Jolie a thousand times over before I'd ever follow you again. You're the reason why Jordan is dead!" Red hairs sprouted along Red's face and hands, as if he could barely contain his inner red wolf.

"Stay calm," Liam commanded, his voice offering no room for argument.

Red snapped his mouth shut, glancing towards his new alpha, before he returned his hateful stare to Renzo.

His quick obedience showed promise for Liam.

"Two then," Renzo growled.

"And me," Mitch said, still standing next to Jordan's parents.

Jordan's father, still holding onto his mate, glared at Renzo. "Both of us, too, and you'd be lucky if I didn't help Liam kill you."

The eyes of everyone in the pack seemed to land on Renzo like hot lasers. He could try to ignore them, but it was clear they were making him sweat from the heat.

"I think you know where this is going," Jolie said. Renzo snapped his attention to her. She shook her head. "Don't make this worse than it already is. You kept the pack relatively peaceful for a lot of years. Just walk away."

Renzo's eyes gleamed blood red. "You want me to just walk away? After he killed Dempsey?"

"You're going to walk away," Liam said, his voice dangerously soft. "Or I'll send you to join him, old man."

That seemed to be the thing that did it. The *old man* comment. Renzo wasn't in his prime anymore. He was still strong enough to hold his own in a fight, but not against a young alpha like Liam.

And he knew it.

The betas who had betrayed Dempsey the first time to follow Liam stepped closer. They still left a wide circle around their new alpha, Jolie, and Renzo, but that single act, one step forward, even from her perspective, solidified them as a unit.

The loyal wolves who would follow and protect their alpha if he needed it.

Jolie could tell Liam didn't need it, but their close proximity made the threat real enough.

Especially for Renzo.

"Do you want to live or do you want to die?" Liam asked. "Because I never forgot what you did to my father, or to my mother."

"So why not kill me right now?" Renzo asked.

Liam sucked back a hard breath.

Jolie's heart pulsed loud and heavy against her ribs. It was almost enough to make her dizziness return.

"Because a good alpha will not kill another man unless he is being attacked first. You give me one reason to do it, and I'll snap your damned neck. Until you do, my hands are tied."

Jolie exhaled hard. She held tightly to Liam's arm, partly for balance, as holding her breath like that hadn't been the best idea in the world, but she couldn't help herself.

He was exactly right. He wouldn't gain the respect of the pack if he murdered Renzo right in front of them, no matter how much Jordan's parents might want him to.

She quickly kissed Liam's arm, wanting to show him how proud she was of him, even if she couldn't say anything about it right now.

Renzo nodded, his eyes still blazing. "Very good. Did *she* tell you that?"

"No," Liam said. "My father did."

A low murmur sounded throughout the pack, the other betas, omegas, mothers, and fathers quietly talking amongst themselves, as if they were watching a soap opera unfolding in front of them.

"You have one hour to collect your things," Liam said. "Josh, Red, and Mitch will watch you. If you try to grab for any weapons, they will stop you and throw your ass out. If you attack them, they have my full authority to beat the living piss out of you so that you're limping out of here, but you will be out of here. Understand?"

Another hard silence. The longest several seconds of waiting Jolie had ever experienced in her entire life.

Renzo's glare didn't vanish, but the boil became a low simmer. "Yes, Alpha."

CHAPTER 29

Jolie had another one of those moments she'd experienced outside of the cabin. What had once been ugly and oppressive suddenly appeared lighter, more hopeful than it had at first glance.

Two days after Renzo packed his things, taking his oldest truck, and drove off to find another pack that would have him, the home that Liam and Jolie spent a good portion of their childhoods in still smelled like him.

Even after all the windows and doors had been left open to air it out.

The smell was starting to weaken, however. Jolie hoped it was just a matter of time before she and her mate would be able to sleep indoors again. Luckily, it hadn't rained, and the nights were beautifully warm.

Even if they hadn't been, Jolie was confident that snuggling into the fur coat of her mate would have kept her warm even in the middle of winter.

She didn't mind sleeping outside with him. There was something innocent about it, about lying against his belly when he was in wolf form, looking up at the stars.

He needed to be outside, she knew that. Over the course of their lives, he was probably not going to be spending every night in a proper bed with her. Jolie might have to invest in a really good tent. That way they could have some privacy when she ultimately convinced him to shift back into his human form and join her.

Those nights would be fun. She couldn't wait for them, but until then, she wouldn't lie. Jolie was starting to get antsy for the touch of her mate.

When he was not in his wolf form, that is.

After another two days, when Jolie thought she was going to have to put her foot down and get Liam to see reason, he shocked her when he took her by her hand and brought her into the home his father and mother shared before his father was killed and he and his mother were thrown out of the house.

Liam walked them into the sitting room with her, that still looked and smelled so different compared to what she'd known as a child. The difference was that she had been in here a few times over the years after Liam had been banished from the pack. The way his eyes scanned the room every time he was in it made it clear he wasn't yet used to what he saw.

He wasn't looking around the room now, however. His nose didn't scrunch in a way that suggested he was being put off by the smell of Renzo and Dempsey in his home either.

No. Instead, his eyes were only on her.

Jolie smiled, feeling a hint of something to come. "We going to spend the night here tonight?"

Liam smiled.

"I mean, I can't think of a better way to get Renzo's scent out of here than replacing it with our own."

Hint. Hint.

Liam sputtered a soft laugh. He briefly looked away from

her, as if he was a shy schoolboy. "Well, if you want. You could have asked and I would have delivered." His warm, powerful palms circled around her waist. The heat of his body, and in his eyes, sent a pleasurable shiver rippling through her skin.

She'd started to think her body had been going to sleep with the lack of attention from her mate, but if that was the case, it was now alive and roaring for attention. Her tail was out and wagging. Since her bandages had come off, that meant her wolf ears, still healing, had also popped out, and they were perky and pointing at the man she wanted.

"I have something else I want to give you instead."

Jolie deflated, her ears falling flat on top of her head, and her tail becoming limp between her legs. "Instead?"

Liam shook his head. "Not the word I meant. But, something I want to give you before we get to that."

"It better be good!" she sputtered. "You can't just tease me and—*oh*."

She exhaled that last word. Softly, slowly, at the sight of the gold band Liam suddenly produced from his back pocket.

She looked at it, and then looked up at him. She *knew* what it was, but her brain wouldn't send the right signals to her mouth to say it out loud.

"You're my mate," Liam said, thankfully speaking up for her. "I know we've talked about a future together, but this…I think this will make it official." Liam wet his lips, and then he dropped down to one knee.

Jolie's hands shot to her mouth, but it wasn't enough to contain the rush of heavy gasping, laughing, and crying that suddenly demanded to escape from her.

Liam took one of her hands, held it, while still holding that ring between his thumb and forefinger. "Be my wife? I don't have a lot to give you right now, but I'm working on it. I'll find something I can do or be other than a strong alpha, and I'll make sure I can provide for you and any pups you give me."

Jolie couldn't see. Her vision blurred as if she'd just sunk under water. She could hardly breathe, and quickly, desperately, she wiped her hands across her eyes to clear her vision. "You're already worth so much to me," she said.

Liam blinked up at her. "Is that a no?"

"*No*! I mean yes! I'm saying yes!"

Jolie fell into his arms, laughing, still crying, and when Liam wrapped his arms around her and lifted her off her feet, she thought he might spin her around like in a romance novel, or the end of a movie. The happy ending.

Except he dropped the ring.

"*Shit!*" Liam dove to grab it before it could roll very far on the hardwood floor. Jolie laughed, still sniffling when Liam grabbed her hand. "Don't want to lose this," he said, putting it on her finger.

"It's beautiful," Jolie said. God, she was a mess. She couldn't stop crying and she could barely control her tears. Happy tears, at least.

"I found it in the safe. It was my mother's."

Jolie's eyes flew wide. She looked at Liam, then her finger, and shook her head.

"Don't even think about saying no," he said with a mock growl. "I can't believe it's been here this whole time, and there's no one better to wear it."

The gleaming diamond and gold band suddenly held so much more meaning to her now, and the meaning she'd thought it had was so powerful. It was like being punched in the heart. That was how happy she was.

"Are you sure?"

Liam nodded, his eyes gleaming as he got to his feet, pulling her closer to his body. "I'm very sure. There's no one better."

Jolie smiled, and she had to wipe her eyes again. She was going to be doing a lot of smiling and crying lately. She could tell.

"Okay, then I'll be happy, and honored, to wear it."

Liam's eyes danced just as his hand cupped her face, and he leaned down to kiss her.

The wild wolf's wife had something of a nice ring to it, she had to admit to that much.

When he pulled back, he had the most peaceful expression she'd ever seen on his face or in his eyes. Her heart spread wings and flew away.

"So, you want to make this house smell like the two of us?"

Jolie nodded. "On every surface."

Liam gripped her hand tightly, the one that now had her new ring on it. "Let's get started."

THE END

FINAL MESSAGE & BONUS SCENE

One last thank you to the amazingly Beautiful Alphas who made this possible :) I wouldn't be doing this without you and you guys make all this so worth it.

IF YOU ARE a Patron and want access to your ebooks at all times, head on over to Patreon.com/MandyRosko and check out the Ebooks Featured Tags section to get your goodies. If you're not a patron, check it out anyway to get these early releases when they come out ;)

FOR A BONUS ENDING SCENE **to The Wild Wolf's Wife, check out Patreon.com/MandyRosko**

IF YOU'RE HAVING trouble getting your books, you can contact me here at a_rosko@hotmail.com

Coming early to Patrons beginning in June, Vampires Don't Share With Dragons Volume One!

ABOUT THE AUTHOR

USA Today Bestselling author Mandy Rosko loves writing paranormal romances with werewolves, dragons and people with special powers. She is the author of the Things in the Night Series, Night and Day, the Dangerous Creatures Series and Alpha Bites. She's also the author of Patreon Reward Books Bad Boy Bear, The Wild Wolf's Wife, and Vampires Don't Share With Dragons.

Patreon.com/MandyRosko
MandyRosko.com
Wattpad.com/user/MandyRosko